D1015754

Death at the Opera

Death at the Opera

John Gano

St. Martin's Press ✖ New York

Library of Congress Cataloging-in-Publication Data

Gano, John.
    Death at the opera / by John Gano.
        p.   cm.
    ISBN 0-312-13961-6
    1. Opera companies—England—Fiction.   I. Title.
PR6057.A47D43   1996
823'.914—dc20   95-30041
                                                                CIP

First published in Great Britain by Macmillan

First U.S. Edition: January 1996
10 9 8 7 6 5 4 3 2 1

Death at the Opera

THE
FLORIA TOSCA
GRAND OPERA COMPANY

present

Don Giovanni

Opera in two Acts by
Wolfgang Amadeus Mozart.
Words by Lorenzo da Ponte

Cast:

Don Giovanni	Bruno Retz
Leporello	Winston Wheeler
Donna Elvira	Jane Nuneham
Donna Anna	Maria Cellini
The Commendatore	Edmund Nuneham
Don Ottavio	Rupert Brock
Zerlina	Isabelle Morny
Masetto	Edmund Nuneham

Director of Music	George Sinclair
Producer & Wardrobe	Jane Nuneham
Stage Manager	Edmund Nuneham

*We gratefully acknowledge the
assistance of Hogene Detergents Ltd in
providing Wardrobe Care on this tour.*

Chapter One

'Ah, ah, *ah*, *ah*, ***AH***, ***AHHH!***'

'No, *no*, *NO*! Use the *back* of the voice, I keep telling you. **Laaahh**! Feel the note. *Feel* it.'

'I am feeling it! Believe me, I'm feeling it.' Maria Cellini, tall, fortyish, stout and yet beautiful in an aquiline way, threw herself angrily down on to her long-suffering *chaise-longue*, and glowered at the man by the piano. A large rubber plant was quietly dying in the corner, and the whole room stank of her scent. Outside, the April sunshine was warming the low suburban streets round Shepherd's Bush, but little of its light was able to penetrate her yellowing lace curtains.

'Shall we try again?' He looked much younger than her, pale, and slight, with large blue eyes and unruly black hair which was falling now across his face. He sounded a note. '*Ah.*'

She stood up. 'Ah, *ah*, ah, ah!'

'Heavens above, Maria! It's ah, *ah*, ah. A natural.' And to make his point clearer, he struck the note on the piano insistently, three or four times.

'Aaaaaaah!' She screamed, her face suddenly flooded with an angry flush of blood. 'I've had enough. *Enough!* Is that clear, Giorgio? To hell with you ... and to hell with Mozart!'

'Please, Maria.' George Sinclair, musical director,

répétiteur and music coach (as well as sole proprietor) of the Floria Tosca Grand Opera Company stood up, his smile quellingly calm. 'The first performance is in five weeks. We need the money.'

'You know what I need!' she said with a sudden change of tone, her great eyes sparkling with mischief. 'Now! I need it now.' She had crossed to him and was pressing him gently against the piano.

'Maria! Please!'

'Look! My breasts are like great melons. They ache for your lips.'

'*Maria!* You promised.'

'Ach!' She turned away in disgust. 'You are useless. A eunuch. You used to be a stallion. You couldn't have enough of me then. It was "Maria, let me undress you!", "Maria, I want your bodee!" See! Here it is, this same Maria, this magnificent body, and you talk only of promises.'

'It's over. You know it's over. It's been over for *six months*. You have to learn your music.'

'And what do you do in that six months? Play with yourself?' Looming over him, she slowly lowered one eyelid in a portentous wink. 'Maria knows what you like.'

'What I like,' said George heavily, 'is for Maria to know "Non mi dir", as Mozart wrote it, and without those awful ornamentations you keep putting in.'

'Grisi,' she said, 'always sang it with the ornamentations.'

'*Grisi!* Grisi was dead before you were born.'

'Grisi was dead before my grandmother was born, but still she sang "Non mi dir" with ornament,' said the big woman, with absolute finality. 'My ornaments are like no other ornaments.'

'You can say that again,' muttered George, turning back to the piano. 'Once more, then?'

'You haven't told me who else is singing?'

2

'Well, Rupert Brock is singing Don Ottavio.'

She smiled with genuine pleasure. 'Dear Rupert. Our voices blend so well.' Then her frown returned. 'Is he still drinking?'

'Hardly at all.'

' "Hardly at all"? So English! What does that mean, truthfully?'

'Yes.' George groaned with exasperation. 'It means, "Yes, he's drinking like a bloody fish." But where else can I find a tenor who doesn't sound like a strangulated donkey to perform in the middle of May, for God's sake? At least Rupert can sing in tune.'

She shrugged expressively. 'Who else?'

'Ed's coming back, and Jane.'

'*No!* Don't tell me they're still together.'

'Of course they're still together. Why wouldn't they be? They're married, aren't they?'

'Oh, Giorgio, *caro*! What a *child* you are. Married? It means nothing ... NOTHING!' Her voice had suddenly acquired a magnificent deep timbre, and she rolled her great eyes to add to the effect. 'Jane is so *greedy*. She must have a man, any man, you know that. Maybe she has had you? Poor George, don't blush. I do not mind. She is no rival for Maria Cellini. So Jane is singing chorus?'

'You know we don't have a chorus,' said George patiently. 'We've never had a chorus, not ever. Jane is singing Donna Elvira, and directing the show, and Ed will stage-manage and sing Masetto and the Commendatore.'

'Such busy, busy people. But you will have to transpose the aria down at least a fourth for her. Poor Jane! She never *can* get above the stave.'

'Talking of which,' put in George adroitly, 'shall we continue?'

*

The Floria Tosca Grand Opera Company had never performed *Tosca*, was far from grand, and the 'company', except when he had a definite engagement, existed only in George Sinclair's head. It was, however, at least true to say that it was exclusively concerned with opera, being one of the many *ad hoc* enterprises which, since the days of Shakespeare, or Blondin, or even Aristophanes, have scraped a living, and sometimes made a fortune, by travelling from place to place offering musical entertainment in return for money or, if all else fails, a bed and some cheap wine. In a good year, some twenty or more performances were presented under its banner; in a bad year, George could fall back on giving piano lessons in Hammersmith, where he had a small basement flat, and spending the summer months playing the upright piano in the bar of the Imperial Esplanade Hotel at Seaford.

After a bleak winter with only a couple of *Così fan tutte*s in a country house outside Godalming to keep him from his Hammersmith pupils, spring had suddenly blossomed by way of the precipitate failure and hasty disappearance of a rival promoter, he of the Imperial Alhambra Opera (known as the 'All Hams' in the trade), whose cheques had suddenly ceased to have any intrinsic value.

No less than twelve clients, having booked the fugitive to present *Don Giovanni* in May and June, were left with their arrangements more or less complete – but without the prospect of a performance actually taking place.

George, having bought their names and addresses for the price of a bottle of Chivas Regal off his competitor's boyfriend, was able to present himself to them as the saviour of the hour, and he now had seven thousand pounds earning interest at his bank, being the balance of the deposits paid (for a second time, as far as the unfortunate clients were concerned). And this was after paying off his overdraft, and making the down payment on two weeks' holiday for one in Venice in early October once the performances were over.

Only for one? After three years in thrall to La Cellini, George had decided, having just passed his thirty-third birthday, that there were substantial advantages to be found in a life of celibacy.

Meanwhile he needed to recruit three more singers: a Zerlina, a Leporello and, most important of all, the Don himself.

Chapter Two

'What will you give us?'

George Sinclair, flanked by Jane Nuneham (already engaged to sing Donna Elvira and act as director), svelte in green silk, and Ed (her husband, the stage-manager cum Masetto cum Commendatore), massive in musty tweed, smiled up at what was likely to be the first of a long line of charmingly helpless, and hopeless, sopranos.

' "Come scoglio",' she replied.

'Next!'

'What . . .?'

'Thank you, dear,' said Ed breezily. 'Will you send the next one in on your way out?'

'But I've come all the way from Glasgow to audition for Donna Elvira! I've spent a bloody fortune on lessons.'

'Part's taken,' snapped Jane, herself the lucky lady. 'Sorry you were troubled.'

'I've prepared "Come scoglio" and having come all the way from Glasgow, I think you ought to hear me.'

Ed stood up. He was built like a gorilla, and could assume the sort of expression that goes with it. '*Addio*,' he said. 'Adieu. *Arrivederci. Auf Wiedersehen.* Farewell. Do I make myself clear, or do you want it tattooed on your buttocks?'

The young woman stuck out her tongue and ran out

of the room. They could hear her complaining shrilly on the other side of the opaque glass door. After a long pause, another young woman, of generous girth, stuck her head round. 'Hello,' she called out nervously. 'I've brought "Parto, parto" . . .'

'Great!' called back Ed, who was getting into his swing. 'You do just that.'

'Where would you like me to stand?'

'No.' Patience was never Jane's strength. 'You've said you're going. Just go.'

'But . . .'

'Look, luv.' Ed was standing up again. 'We're looking for a Zerlina. You're the wrong shape, and you've got the wrong voice. Otherwise you're perfect. NEXT!'

'Ed.'

'Yes, George?'

The embarrassed impresario was rubbing his left ear, an invariable sign of mental disturbance. 'I think you should leave the decisions about who we hear to me,' he said. 'I greatly appreciate your frankness, but I don't like being so hard on these girls. They have put a lot of effort into coming here, you know.'

'So have we,' snapped Jane. 'The day you pay us for our time auditioning, that's the day I'll sit till the cows come home, listening to as many fat duds as you like to pay me to. Next!'

The next singer to audition threw the double doors of the church hall open and marched over to their table. He was black, six foot tall, and weighed upwards of 220 pounds.

'Hi.'

'Hi,' they all said in unison.

'I'd like to sing "La calumnia" for you. Any objections?'

'Please go ahead,' said George, while the others nodded enthusiastically. 'I don't think we have a copy of your CV.'

'No,' said the giant. 'You don't. It's my voice I'm selling, not my autobiography.'

'Oh, quite,' said George. 'Fine. Please go ahead.'

While Mr Sumption, the grey-haired old session pianist (at eleven pounds an hour plus packet of Rothmans and his tube fare), struck up the opening chord, the three of them settled down with pencil and paper to assess their newest applicant by means of George's patent formula: A to D for singing and one to four on looks.

Anyone scoring A for singing was hired on the spot, the Bs were listed and kept in reserve, Cs they smiled at and Jane would, later, offer them vocal tuition at her special introductory rates. As for the Ds, these were cut off in mid-aria and strongly encouraged to try the Operamobile Company, a rival concern, for whom George would assure them they were 'uniquely qualified'.

Much the same went for looks. The twos were hired, the threes kept in reserve and the fours directed to the nearest circus. And the ones? A rare category indeed, but one which temporarily halted the whole process since it was a privilege only extended to a singer whom one of the panel had conceived an immediate and urgent desire to bed at the earliest opportunity.

'... *La Calumnia* ... – *è un venti-ce-e-ello* ...'

'What do you think?' whispered Ed after a bit. He never liked to commit himself to an opinion without first consulting Jane.

George had already awarded an A for singing. 'Would you like to be the one to say no?' he whispered back, interested. 'Because ...' He broke off on seeing he was being watched by the singer. They sat in perfect silence until the end.

'Well?' The man's truculence had entirely gone now. In some strange way – despite the aggression implicit in the aria he had chosen – the making of music had calmed his spirit and left him docile and modest where before he had been thoroughly intimidating.

'That was wonderful,' said George, who meant it.

'Yeh,' said Ed, keeping one eye half cocked in the hope of some message from his wife, who never thanked him for disagreeing with her own strongly articulated opinions. She seemed in the grip of some new emotion which he couldn't quite identify.

'Leporello, I think,' said George.

'I'd rather sing the Don,' said the man, with something of his old spirit returning.

'You would shine in either,' said Jane unexpectedly.

'Nevertheless, I can offer you Leporello,' said George firmly. 'Twelve shows for two hundred and five pounds, including all rehearsals, and there might be some petrol money in it if you run a car.'

'Doesn't seem much.'

'Hark at Pavarotti!' shouted Ed, who had given him a two D.

'He means two hundred and five pounds each show,' put in Jane, standing up. 'Twelve times two hundred and five.'

'Oh!' The man's face cleared. 'That's better. Do we get a contract?'

'Gentleman's honour,' murmured George diffidently.

'And which of us is supposed to be the gent?' enquired his new Leporello, to general laughter. 'When do I start?'

'What's your name?' said Jane softly.

'Winston Wheeler.'

'Do you have a work permit?' asked the cautious Ed, who didn't much care for his wife's new attitude. He wanted to see what she had written, but she, being prudent, had covered her score-sheet with her hand.

'Why? Where are we going? Bosnia?'

'Depends on your passport,' muttered Ed sullenly.

'Oh?' He opened his mouth very wide and laughed. 'That's British, mate. I was born in leafy Huddersfield.'

Someone started banging on the outside door. 'Yes,' said George. 'We must get on. Leave your address with Jane here. We start rehearsing as soon as we've got a complete cast. Next week probably.'

'Goodbye, then,' growled Ed.

'See you!' Winston waved a cheery hand, and ran out, leaving Jane leaning weakly against the table.

'Wow!' she said.

'*Wow!*' mimicked her infuriated husband. '*WOW!*'

'Let's see who's next,' suggested George quickly. 'Jane, will you let the next one in?'

'Certainly.' She sighed, and walked over to open the door to a young woman wrapped in a thick overcoat several sizes too large for her and wearing, of all things, a red sou'wester, which she shyly removed to reveal long shining hair of the palest blonde.

'What had you planned to sing?' asked Jane sharply.

' "Batti, batti" or "Vedrai carino"?' The young woman smiled, showing sharp little teeth.

'Perfect!' said George, smiling. 'It's a Zerlina we're actually looking for.'

'Oh?' She began unwrapping the coat. Ed's jaw dropped. She was wearing a short dress of clinging black silk jersey, which showed everything a red-blooded audience might want to see, and quite a lot besides.

George gulped, and, covering his paper with his hand, wrote a small 1 with flowery tails.

St Seraphina's, West Fulham, was a church wholly lacking charm. Its modest classical predecessor, much loved by its congregation, had been demolished in the sixties and replaced by a strangely hostile pyramid of yellow brick. With its attenuated spire and thin mean windows, it gave off an air of sullen menace, by no means disarmed by the current pastor, a grim friar of titanic girth much given to 'speaking in tongues'. But if the congregation, shrunk now to a few youths, and old Mr Biddulph, the churchwarden, produced little in the way of an income, the church hall, a splendid remnant in the earlier style, complete with coffered ceiling and pilasters, where the auditions were taking place, continued to earn good money thanks to its excellent acoustics and sympathetic interior. One hundred and twenty pounds per day was the going rate, though George had got it slightly cheaper by dressing down, in dungarees, and pleading extreme poverty.

He was still gulping in the new soprano's measurements when he felt someone push against his arm. It was a little old lady, her white hair neatly tied back in a bun, and she settled herself comfortably on Jane's chair.

'Lovely day,' she said, companionably.

George stared at her. 'We're holding auditions,' he said. 'For an opera.'

'That's nice,' said the old lady peaceably. 'I can't sing myself, but I do like a nice tune.' She was clearly there to stay.

'Are you ready?' The blonde girl was staring at them. She spoke with quite a strong French accent.

'Please.' Surely . . . yes!

The old lady had a *dog*, a little Sealyham, perched on her foot. George caught Ed's eye. The big man was speechless.

'Vedrai car-in-o-° . . .' The blonde could sing! What a find. George couldn't take his eyes off her, for all that an unpleasant smell was coming his way from his neighbour, or his neighbour's dog. He added an A to her score.

'Lovely voice,' confided the old lady graciously, this time to Ed.

'Yes, indeed,' he replied gruffly.

'I hope she comes often.'

'So do I.'

'You never know where you are in these modern services, do you?'

'I suppose not.'

'Excuse me.' The blonde had had enough. 'Is that all you want to hear?'

George stood up, casting a helpless glance at Ed. 'Yes,' he said. 'That's perfect. We're having a little difficulty ...' He rolled his eyes sideways to try to indicate the old lady, '... but the job's yours ... if you want it?' How could she, when the whole world must be at her feet?

'Really?' she said, and ran her tongue lightly over her lips. 'Zerlina?'

'Yes.'

'How many shows?'

'Twelve, at the moment.'

'No chorus work?'

'No.'

'No understudying?'

'No.'

'What's the catch?'

'We pay two hundred and five pounds per show, but that includes unlimited rehearsal time and music calls.'

'I've worked for less!'

'Do I have your CV?'

'No.' She walked up to him and handed over a sheet of paper. 'Here it is.' He stared sightlessly at it. 'Other way up.'

'Isabelle Morny,' he read. 'You trained at the Royal College?' He looked up, to meet two very direct, and smiling, blue eyes. Susceptibility in men was not, for her, a new sensation.

'Uh-huh. What about you?'

'Me?' It was so long ago he could scarcely remember. 'Royal Northern. With Hartley Barttelot.'

12

'Piano, then.'

'You know him?'

'George!' It was Jane, who had come over from the piano. 'We do have another twenty people building up in an increasingly disorderly queue outside.'

'Yes,' he said guiltily. 'Of course. So! Isabelle's joining us.'

'Good,' said Jane, smoothing the green dress.

'Good,' chimed in the old lady, while Ed contented himself with stroking the dog, and imagining that it was Isabelle's supple body already responding to his touch.

'I'm so sorry!' Ushering out Isabelle as fast as she could, Jane had rushed out into the corridor where the other singers were waiting. 'We're getting through as quick as we can.'

'I've got a show tonight,' muttered one man.

'And you are?'

He gave her his card: 'Bruno Retz. *Primo baritono assoluto.*' A tall man, with broad shoulders and dense black hairs curling out of an open-neck shirt.

'You'd better go next,' she said. 'I should warn you. We've got an interloper on the panel. Some nutter.'

'Oh?' The man shrugged, letting his eyes drop briefly to examine her figure. He had the thinnest of moustaches and his eyes shone yellow in the half-light. Walking confidently through the door, he advanced towards the table, and the three figures behind it: on the right, a big bruiser in tweeds, in the middle an old lady with a lopsided smile, and on the left, an untidy dark man, imperfectly shaved, holding a Sealyham on his lap. Nutters, all three, by his reckoning. As per usual in this business.

'I'm Bruno,' he said.

'Would you ever be able to sing the Don?' asked the man struggling with the dog.

'I do,' said Bruno firmly. 'I *do* sing the Don.'

' "Finch'o dal vino", then?' said the same man, having now firmly pushed his dog back under the table.

'Suits me,' said Bruno. The beefy man at the other end was turning puce. Who *were* these clowns? The sexy number in green silk settled back by the piano and the grey-haired old geezer at the keys took him by surprise by racing into the introduction before he was ready.

Undismayed, he spun on his heels, throwing out one arm while using the other to balance, and tore into the aria, grateful, as always, that the many months spent learning his technique always kept him with plenty of air at his command.

Though singing in Italian, his mind was always instantly translating the ideas into English, so that, in boasting how he would bowl over another ten women before the day was out, he twinkled roguishly first at the sexy bit (who twinkled back with practised aplomb) and then, since she seemed to be in charge, at the old biddy behind the table. To his alarm, she started nodding vigorously. Surely she wasn't expecting . . .! It was over, and the man with the dog applauded loudly.

'Great,' he said. 'Splendid. You are . . .?'

'I told you. Bruno. Bruno Retz. You've got my CV under your biscuits. There.' He pointed at a now crumbed and crumpled sheet of paper covered in type-script, a sheet that contained the brief triumphs and omitted the dreary disappointments of eleven years hard slog since he had left school to try his luck at music college.

'The Don it is, then,' said George with a triumphant sigh. 'Rehearsals in ten days. Be sure you know it.'

'English or Italian?'

'Eh?'

'Do you perform the piece in English, or in Italian?'

'Italian, of course,' said George grandly.

'And could I have an advance?'

'An advance?' Ed's mouth had dropped open. 'Like money, you mean?'

'Yes, please,' said Bruno with a simple smile. 'Because (a) I need to buy a score, and (b) I need to eat if I'm to be heard. Oh, and (c) I'm broke. A hundred quid would cover it.'

George felt in his pocket and brought out a wad of twenty-pound notes. 'On account,' he said, genially peeling off five, 'and strictly returnable if you don't know your recitatives, right?'

'Right!' Bruno, who hadn't expected to get anything, was now regretting he hadn't asked for more.

As for Ed, he was positively sweating with rage. 'A hundred quid,' he almost shouted when Bruno had left. 'That's the last you'll see of him.'

'It's worth it,' said George with all the confidence of a man in credit with his bankers. 'He sang that really well.'

'And he looked the part,' murmured Jane, who enjoyed teasing her mercurial husband.

'Thank you so much,' said a voice behind them. The little old lady had gathered up her dog and was poised in the doorway. 'I found it most uplifting.'

'Same time next week, dear,' shouted Ed, adding in a furious undertone, 'Barmy old bitch!' as she disappeared into the gloom. 'NEXT!' They settled down to hear the other hopefuls outside. After all, who knew if they might need a few Bs in reserve, or if Jane could find some Cs to boost the fragile marital income.

Chapter Three

While George was searching for his cast, Mary Bolitho, wife of Colonel Billy Bolitho, of Bolitho Court, Coombe Constantine, in the county of Cornwall, was searching for her spectacles. A short thin woman, with grey hair and an enchanting smile, she had managed to regain her seat on the sofa and was vainly feeling round her feet with loose feathery gestures when a voice from the window called out, 'Other side! To your left!'

'What?' She screwed up her eyes, but it was no good. The whole room was just a blur.

'Your glasses, woman! They're on the floor to your *left*!'

Forty years in the Duke of Cornwall's Hussars had left their mark on Colonel Bolitho, a man for whom every open space seemed a parade ground, and who operated on the principle that the louder you said something, the more likely it was to be understood.

'There they are.' Gratefully she picked them up, and her husband's face swam into focus. 'You're looking very hot, dear.'

'Hot' hardly did justice to the Colonel's face, coloured as it was from a palette exclusively composed of rich gentians and angry mauves. 'Just been weeding the border,' he said, adopting a heroic expression. 'For your bloody nurses.'

16

'*Such* a good cause,' she murmured. 'Is it time for your drink?'

The old soldier shook his head. 'Another seven minutes,' he said. '*Another seven minutes.*'

'Yes, dear. I want you to help me with some envelopes after that.' She gave him her warmest smile.

'Envelopes?' He had learnt to distrust that smile, though it never failed to melt his heart.

'Yes, dear. For the opera.'

Those three little words. How harmless they sounded, yet what a clangorous vision of smoke-filled battle they evoked. The Colonel had fought on many fields. He had fought hand-to-hand with turbaned tribesmen in the blood-soaked jungle north of Oudipore. He had slugged it out in the desert, shell for shell, with Italian tanks among the wadis of Bebi-al-Khum, and he had silently strangled two German sentries on the banks of the Rhine. But never had he fought such a dogged unyielding campaign as against his daughter's idea to hold an opera in the house. In Bolitho itself, blest haunt of ancient peace and of yet more ancient Bolithos. Let his distant cousins down round Penzance do what they chose, he would guard this northern redoubt of his great family against shrill painted bumboys and who knew what else. *Opera!* Every engagement on the subject had been closely and bloodily fought, and yet the outcome had gone against him in the end, as he had always known it would.

He and his wife had but one child, Rose, heiress to the name, and house, of Bolitho, and the few hundred precipitous acres of scrubby grass and tangled woodland that surrounded it, a small promontory that, poking its sharp rocky nose inquisitively out into the Atlantic surf, was marked on atlases as Bolitho Point, while known more familiarly to the locals as 'Bolly's Prick'.

The house itself was four-square round two small

17

cobbled courts, and approached by a third gravelled court open on one side and distinguished by a heavy Victorian *porte-cochère* large enough to take a petrol tanker. Rebuilt in the reign of Mary Tudor, the low hunched stone dwelling, two storeys of weathered grey granite, seemed to crouch round its central courtyard, its two bows united by a low white colonnade facing the sea, and a tall Victorian conservatory tacked onto its southern wall. Monmouth was said to have stopped here, just days before the fatal Battle of Sedgmoor, and Judge Jeffreys too, a few months later, enjoying old Squire Bolitho's Madeira before hanging him in chains to rot at the High Tor crossroads. It was the Squire's son, 'Long Tom' Bolitho, who had undermined his descendant, the Colonel, by knocking three rooms of the old house into one great 'saloon', paid for with the money he had brought back from Barbados – and in the process forming a room large enough for an opera.

'What's wrong with the Coliseum?' the Colonel said, seeing that Rose had joined them. 'Or the King's Theatre in Plymouth? Why here?'

'Dear Dad! You don't understand, do you?' Rose Bolitho took after her mother, being scarcely more than five feet two, with short dark hair, a slim figure and a warm, Mediterranean complexion. 'You'll love it. Think! *Don Giovanni*, and in your own home.'

'If I'd wanted that,' he said fiercely, 'I'd have gone to live in bloody Covent Garden. If it's such a good idea, why don't the Kempes do it at Carclew?'

'They do.'

'Oh?' It was always like that, arguing with Rose. She *always* managed to talk her way past him. The trouble was, he doted on her. She was everything he would have wanted in a son – sharp, hard-working, a fine shot, transparently honest and not afraid to fight her corner. Deep inside himself, he wanted her to win. Deep inside herself, she knew that too. Now nearly thirty-two, she had a part-time job in London, running the central office of the St Osyth Hospices Trust. This occupied her from Tuesday morning to Thursday afternoon. The rest of the week she spent with her parents, who, having come to parenthood very late, and now being in their seventies, longed for her to marry and fill the old house with squalling baby half-Bolithos.

'I still don't see how you're going to get a hundred-and-fifty people into the Saloon, and an opera on top.' He had pulled out his pipe and was trying to light it, succeeding only in singeing his thick grey moustache.

'Let me.' Rose leant out of the window, took the box of matches from his hand and applied a flame to the pipe. He drew some short grateful puffs and let out a stream of grey-blue smoke.

'There won't be any guests if you don't help me with these envelopes,' added Mary, coming to the window.

'Good thing too.' Some of the fumes went the wrong way, and he started to cough. 'God! What's that noise?'

'The piano tuner,' said Rose, laughing. 'He said he wanted me to check if the thing can be tuned. Heaven only knows when it was last played.'

'He said? *Who* said?'

'Mr Sinclair. The opera man. He's coming down tomorrow to check.'

'Very good of him, I'm sure. Your grandmother was a fine pianist,' sniffed the Colonel, sucking in some soothing smoke. 'Nothing wrong with that piano. Made by some bloody German, of course.'

'*Will* you come and help with these envelopes?' said his wife. 'The post goes at one o'clock, and I do want to see Mrs Tregeare about the chops.'

'First things first,' cried the Colonel, tapping his watch triumphantly. 'Twelve fifteen. Time for a bracer!'

Chapter Four

Home for George Sinclair was a rented basement flat off Hammersmith Broadway. Steep area steps led down and into a dingy hallway, scarcely three feet across, which offered two choices: a frosted glass door into a living-room-cum-kitchen at the front, or a pine door into a bedroom-cum-bathroom at the rear.

Yet the result was considerably more than its constituent parts. By the use of bright colours, here lemon lacquered walls, there scarlet silk sheets, he had managed to make this subterranean den into a welcoming blaze of brightness, cooled by a full-size plaster cast of Tallentini's *Venus Flagrans* sprawled invitingly on a wooden plinth in the bedroom bay window, and, in the living room, a tall blue and white glazed Viennese stove.

Although innocent of heat, serving instead as a highly efficient store for his precious collection of fine wines, this last, as curvaciously rococo as the Venus, and, at nearly eight feet tall, all but brushing the ceiling, was his sole inheritance from his mother, an Austrian soprano who had died when he was only five.

His father, one among the many *répétiteurs* working between the Royal Opera House and wherever else he could scrape a living, had only to see her first performance as Sophie in *Rosenkavalier* under the baton of the great Szelko to know that this woman was The One.

Lowly as his status was, he had triumphed, even though gossip whispered that others higher, *much* higher, had triumphed too. They had married and she had promptly produced a son, George. And if gossip, indefatigable as ever, had continued to whisper that the infant George's looks favoured the great Szelko, and that Mr Sinclair, unencumbered by a wife, had been willing to swallow anything to possess the lissom Maria Theresa Sagan, certainly no one was complaining. Sinclair got the girl, Maria Theresa got a roof over her head (and the stove from the set of Act Two as a wedding present from Szelko), and George got a name.

As for Szelko, fat, smiling, heavy-lidded Szelko, he returned to the Austrian Alps, and looked around for another nubile young Sophie. At his age, and with his girth, it was the easiest way to find companionship, especially as he owned a company that made reproduction rococo stoves.

Flinging himself down on the disordered scarlet sheets, George closed his eyes and tried to remember exactly what Isabelle, the blonde soprano, had looked like. Sharp blue eyes, so pale, thin, skinny even, but with rounded thighs and a taut bottom only just covered by that indecent little dress. There was something about her, a hunger in her wide lips and languorous lids, a hint even of greed, that gave her a sexuality that had left him gasping with desire. To feel her writhing under him! Here! To . . .

The telephone rang, shocking him from his trance. 'Mr Sinclair?'

'Yes,' he said, catching his breath guiltily.

'This is Rose Bolitho speaking. I wanted to check if you knew your way here tomorrow.'

'Yes,' he said. 'Thank you. I was going to take the A30 all the way to Launceston and then head north on the B3254.'

'Oh, no!' she said, laughing. 'That'll take you a month. Take the M4 past Bristol, and then south on the M5. You come off at Junction 27 into Tiverton and then follow the A3072 nearly to the bitter end, forking north to Kilkhampton and then follow the signs past Deanshanger to Tredinnick. Coombe Constantine is just six miles on from there, on the Penwillow road. Have you got that?'

'Junction 27, A3072, Kilkhampton and then on to Tredinnick.' He was scribbling hastily on a scrap of newspaper. 'Six miles past Tredinnick. And the house?'

'There's a big pair of stone gateposts opposite the post office. I don't think you'll miss it. Will you stay for lunch?'

'That's very kind,' he said politely, wondering how to refuse. 'How long will it take?'

'About three and three-quarter hours, traffic permitting. If you leave London at eight, you'll have plenty of time to look round, have a nice quiet lunch with us, and be back in London by teatime.'

Teatime? He shook his head unbelievingly. *Teatime?* What sort of people rationed *tea*, of all things, to one period of the day? Or did she mean tea as in supper, north country style? It takes all sorts, he told himself, while quietly disengaging himself from the conversation. 'Great.'

'See you then.'

'I'll look forward to it.'

'Sure you've got the way now?'

'Yes, thank you.'

'Goodbye,' she said at last.

'Goodbye.' He put the receiver down before she could qualify her farewell. Some people never could leave go. Which brought him back to Maria.

Maria! He closed his eyes in despair. He was torn between anger and the most poignant sympathy for his one-time mistress. Indeed she stirred other emotions too: admiration for her magnificent voice, amusement at her outrageous vanity, respect for her meticulous musicality. But the one emotion he could not rekindle was the very one that she most hoped for: desire for that voluptuous polygonal mass of heaving flesh which once had enslaved him. How sad, he thought, shaking his head, that human passion withers so unexpectedly, and with such finality. Yet what could he do? Surely it was the ultimate betrayal, to use a willing body as a convenience, counterfeiting passion with the coldest of calculations? Or had she so abandoned her self-respect that even that poor substitute for their former ardour would be preferable to the present impasse? I *could* do it, he thought ruefully, reluctantly aware of a masculine hunger. I *could* do it with a one-legged goat for that matter! But poor Maria.

Soon it would be time to open a bottle. The '66 Chateau Talbot, perhaps. Bought for thirty-six pounds the case at an auction ten years ago, this was his last bottle. However good or bad his circumstances, he had always kept to his self-imposed rule: never pay more than twenty pounds, never sell. He'd gone straight from college into the wine trade, spending three years at, or under, the feet of an Old Harrovian with a ripe complexion and an even riper sense of business ethics. That was the time of the great 'wine investment' boom, when punters were buying wine to appreciate in value rather than at their tables.

An affable rogue, his employer had cheerfully sold and stored first growth clarets to his prosperous contacts, and then just as cheerfully sold the same bottles at auctions under his wife's name, keeping just enough stock in case one of the unfortunates should wish to taste his 'investment'. Then, when the market dropped, the remaining stock was 'bought' by his wife thus concealing any trace of wrong-doing and the pair of them retired to Bordeaux where they had a number of contacts with reason to be grateful. All this George had observed before deciding to leave the wine trade.

The telephone rang again.

'Mr Sinclair?'

'Yes?' Surely it was *she*? And he didn't mean Maria.

'This is Isabelle Morny.' YES! 'I wondered if there was any chance of a session on music before rehearsals start? If that weren't a nuisance . . .?' Her voice tailed away, hesitantly.

'No.' He had deliberately held back, slowing his response to hide any undue enthusiasm. 'I think that is a good idea. Yes. I do.' What was the *matter* with him?

'I'm all right on the arias. It's the ensembles I'm a bit shaky on.'

'I understand.' *Her! Here!* 'When would be convenient for you?'

'Oh . . .' She laughed nervously. 'I thought I should fit in with you . . .'

Tonight? Now? 'What about tomorrow at seven p.m.?'

'Yes!' she said. 'That's fine for me.'

'Me too,' he said. 'I have to go down to Cornwall to see a house where we're performing. But I'll be back by then. Have you got the address?'

'Yes,' she said, sounding suddenly shy. 'It's in the phone book.'

'Of course.' Abruptly, she rang off, leaving his mind full of thoughts as burning scarlet as his sheets.

Chapter Five

'Inspector the Marquess of East Finchampstead adjusted his impeccably knotted silk foulard tie and grinned at the Chief Constable. "It's quite OK, Tuffy," he said, watching the other lazily, "I'll smoke little Rubinstein out of his lair. Remember how we used to outsmart the rascals in Dr McWhirter's House Team?" The Chief Constable gasped. "Not a bifurk?" The other man nodded, bathing his chief in the emerald green light from his sparkling eyes.'

In his leather-hung Library, Colonel Bolitho was, as was usual on a Saturday morning, reading aloud the latest book sent down from his London bookseller while his wife knitted patiently, and Rose kept as still as she could.

'That makes two,' she said suddenly.

The Colonel sighed and put down the book. 'Two what?'

'Two marquesses in one squad. Even the Sergeant's a bloody baronet, for God's sake.'

'Rose, please.' Mrs Bolitho's voice when remonstrating always held a slightly tired timbre. The Colonel on the other hand rather enjoyed his daughter's salty language.

'No, but seriously,' went on Rose, 'who wrote this lunacy? The editor of *Debrett*?'

'It came highly recommended. It'll get better, I'm sure.'

'It better had.'

He picked up the book.

'The red Bakelite telephone suddenly rang. The Chief Constable answered it, and immediately sprang to his feet. "Yes. Yes." His voice betrayed sudden nervousness. At last he handed it to Sandy. "It's for you," he said. "Your mother." '

It was nearly eleven. And George – who had, unusually for him, managed to leave early, so keen was he to get back in good time to prepare for Isabelle – was sitting staring at the back of a transit truck. He ground his teeth with rage. It was not that the truck, as trucks go, was especially offensive. It was more that this truck wouldn't go. In fact, he had been staring at it for nearly half an hour. And the way things were progressing on the M5, he was expecting to stare at it for the rest of the day.

'No,' he shouted at the top of his voice, 'No, I don't care that you're ill. I wouldn't care two hoots if you were dying. Just move the bloody truck!' It was one of his failings that he was prone to fight imaginary battles in his head, battles that in real life never came near to being offered.

To his right was a metal hoarding advertising the telephone number of a 'Cone Hotline'. What for? To beg for more? To shout abuse in a patient ear? To tell them what intimate horrors he would perpetrate if he ever met Sir Robert McAlpine, or any of his sons, or even the most remote and forgotten members of the road contractor's family? Just a distant cousin would do. Why dig up a motorway just at the start of the holiday season? In particular, why dig up this one? Today?

'*Isabelle!*' He groaned aloud, his mind whirling with thoughts of her naked body, her flesh, her touch... Surely... perhaps... *please*...

'Were you giving any thought to moving, or are you happy here?' He started, and turned to find a man with a strange smile leaning against his door, peering through the half-open window. 'Perhaps it's the view?'

'Er...' There was suddenly no sign of the lorry in front. Miraculously, the traffic had cleared, and the other two lanes were streaming away, with some cars already accelerating into the empty lane ahead of him. Somewhere behind them someone was leaning on their horn.

'Just so as we have some idea.' The man's tone held silken menace, for all he continued to smile the same quizzical smile.

'So sorry.' George threw the little 2CV grindingly into gear. 'I was day-dreaming.'

'When you're ready.' The man walked back to his car, as George accelerated shakily south.

He drove as fast as he dared but, even so, it was almost one before he spotted the fat stone pillars that squatted on either side of a pitted gravel track opposite the thatched post-office-cum-village-store of Coombe Constantine. The drive wound through a jungle of laurels before suddenly dropping through a belt of stunted firs and there, hedged in by more laurels, he came face to face with the hunched stone façade of Bolitho Court.

'My God!' he said, shaking his head. 'To think of someone choosing to live here.' Nevertheless, he climbed out of the car and hurried over to the tall wooden door. It looked as if it should have had a great metal knocker, preferably with a portcullis thrown in. Beside this portal of doom he found a large brass knob, which he pushed hard. Nothing happened.

Indoors the reading continued. Mary Bolitho had

long since fallen asleep, soothed by the steady drone of her husband's special reading voice.

> '... Despite the height of the old tower, Sandy East Finchampstead was able to scramble up the thick trunk of the ivy. Somewhere, behind that heavy grille, his mother, Lady Muriel East Finchampstead, lay at the mercy of the rascally Rubinstein—'

'No!' said Rose, interrupting. 'That's so ridiculously wrong.' Her father laid down the book again with another sigh. 'His mother could be called Lady East Finchampstead. She could be called Muriel, Lady East Finchampstead. She could even, assuming as I think we may, with this author, that her father was at least an earl, be called Lady Muriel Something-Quite-Else if she had remarried to Mister or, more probably, Sir Whocares Something-Quite-Else. What she should *never* be called is Lady Muriel East Finchampstead.'

'Then at least we know who didn't write it,' said her father.

'Who's that?'

'The editor of *Debrett*.' And he positively shook with laughter at his own little joke. 'To continue—' He wiped his eyes with his red-spotted silk handkerchief.

'Is this man ever coming?' interrupted Mary Bolitho, who had been woken by his guffaws. 'It's after one o'clock. I'd better tell Mrs Tregeare to take the beef out.'

'Just wait till I finish the chapter, will you?' The Colonel's voice held something of a rasp, and his wife subsided with a gentle smile.

> '... Raising his face cautiously above the ivy-mantled sill, he found himself staring straight into his mother's startled grey eyes. "How de do?" said Lady Muriel.'

28

' "How de do!" ' shrieked Rose, feigning outrage.
' "*How de do?*" Nobody says, "How de do"!'

'Well, I didn't write the bloody book,' retorted her
father angrily. 'And if . . .' Luckily, at that moment, they
heard the doorbell begin to clang, activated at last by
George deciding to pull the knob, instead of pushing
at it.

There was some scuffling outside, a knock, and then
a little old bent woman with piercing dark eyes, rheumy
cheeks and sparse white hair peered round the door.
'Will you see a Mr Sinclair? I think he's the young man
you're expecting for lunch. He says he's very late.'

'He is!' said the Colonel. 'Very late indeed.'

'Ask him to come in, please,' put in Mrs Bolitho
hurriedly.

'And shall I put the beef in?'

Mrs Bolitho stared at her. 'Put it *in*? I told you to
put it in at noon.'

Mrs Tregeare pursed her lips. Her white hair held a
single strand which had remained obstinately black, as
if defying the power of nature. 'Mrs Bolitho,' she said,
her voice deep and resonant, 'you told me to put it in
when the young man arrived.'

'Yes, yes. But we were expecting him before noon.'

'Well, he's here now, so I'll go and put the beef in,'
said the old crone triumphantly. 'If I turn the gas up,
it'll be ready all the sooner!' And she disappeared
behind the door, her place being taken by the apologetic
figure of George Sinclair.

'I'm *so* sorry,' he said. 'The traffic was awful.'

'I'm Mary Bolitho,' said his hostess hurrying forward,
'and this is my husband, Billy.' The Colonel stood his
ground and glowered. 'And my daughter, Rose.'

'How de do,' said Rose demurely, one eye on her
father, but if she was expecting an explosion, she was
disappointed.

To George's mystification, the old soldier let out a loud laugh and clapped his daughter on the back. 'All right,' he said. 'All right. I've got the message. Now let me find our guest a drink. Glass of sherry, or some whisky and soda?'

'Er ...'

'Tell us what you'd really like,' said Mrs Bolitho kindly.

'Well...' George felt warmed by her sympathetic smile. 'I don't suppose you have any white wine?'

Rose, spotting the change in her father's expression, rushed forward. 'Of course we do,' she said, quelling the mutinous Colonel with her own version of his fierce black stare. 'You must be *exhausted* after your drive. Sit down and chat to my parents while I get you a glass of wine.'

'From the rack at the bottom of the cellar stairs,' her father called after her, anxiously.

'We're so looking forward to the opera,' said Mary Bolitho. 'Do take a seat.'

'Thank you.' George stared about him, trying to avoid his host's bulging eyes. The room was very obviously the Library, with its tall bookcases, their glass doors guarding row upon row of dull leather-bound books: *A Naturalist's Cornwall* in twenty, even thirty, volumes, *The Hurlingham Guide to Coursing*, and so on. Although cold even for the end of April, the huge stone fireplace was innocent of logs, and indeed the whole house exuded an ambience of clinging damp, that special English-country-house micro-climate which battles so successfully for survival over the most modern and combative systems of central heating.

This was an atmosphere to which George had had to accustom himself, as impresario to that equally resilient species, *Homo impervious*, the human inhabitants who formed the largest group of fauna able to survive in

English country mansions under such inauspicious circumstances.

The Bolithos' closest neighbours, the bats, mice, shrews, *rats* even, spiders, woodlice, bluebottles, woodworm, death-watch beetles and plain old-fashioned carpet mites, all of them maintained thriving colonies in this, as in so many other similar big old houses. *They* had nothing to fear from bank managers or from bookmakers, or even from the deceptively small brown envelopes of the Inland Revenue. Their diet stood ready about them in the rotting curtains, the weathered (but not unpalatable) beams and floorboards, and the scraps that Mrs Tregeare, whose eyes were no longer as sharp as in her youth, often left lying about on the kitchen and pantry floors. And if they were occasionally discomfited by the annual streams of melting ice and snow which always seeped under the decayed leads on the sagging roof, flowing promiscuously down behind the wainscots and bringing new life to despairing fungi, then they kept it to themselves.

'Here we are!' The daughter was back, a pretty young woman, dark and slim, with something of Maria about those warm cheeks and fine dark eyes, though half the height. He shrugged. To hell with fine dark eyes when one is looking forward to entering upon the conquest of a woman like Isabelle.

'Isn't this what you wanted?' asked Rose, misunderstanding his gesture. She had rather taken to this awkward newcomer, with his vague yet confident demeanour, and his hopelessly ill-fitting clothes. Chopin dressed by Oxfam and shaved by Blind Pew. A little feminine moulding, and who knew how he might blossom? It was her greatest failing, this tendency to fall immediately in love with men whom she believed could be changed for the better, regardless of the results of her previous endeavours.

'Yes. Yes, it is.' George took a swig from his glass and gasped. 'But this is wonderful,' he said. 'Wonderful.'

'Really?' The Colonel looked up, suspiciously.

'In fact . . .' George sniffed it. 'Could it possibly be a Le Montrachet . . . say . . . 1986 . . . no, sorry, surely it's the 1978?'

'I . . .' For once the Colonel was lost for words. Only his tortured look conveyed to his daughter the depth of her treachery.

'Is that good?' she enquired with an innocent air.

'That's so very generous of you,' George said to the unhappy Colonel. 'Very generous indeed. Aren't you going to have some yourself?'

'No.'

'Daddy sticks to sherry before lunch,' said Rose helpfully. 'Perhaps he'll have some this evening . . . if there's any left.'

'Now, darling.' Mrs Bolitho was a seasoned weather expert, but even the stupidest student would have spotted 'hurricane' written all over the Colonel's empurpled face in block capitals. 'I think it's time to show Mr Sinclair the Saloon.'

'Yes, please,' said George, standing up. After all, he was worrying about the drive back towards London, towards Isabelle. And it was already half-past one. What time did these people have lunch?

Nevertheless he patiently followed the two women through the hall, with its gruesome cases of stuffed animals and, mounted up on the walls behind, the bare reproachful antlers of stags slaughtered by the Colonel and his forebears, Bolithos immemorial, huntsmen all. A low door led into a long arched corridor which led round one side of the inner quadrangle, glimpses of which were given by tiny pointed windows let into the bulging white-washed walls.

At last another low door, of unvarnished oak studded with iron bolts, led into a small room hung with mouldy tapestries.

'Here we are,' said Mrs Bolitho.

'Here?' George stared. The room was barely twelve feet square.

'Your "green room". Where you change. That awful Mr Boden said there'd have to be a "green room". He was very happy with this.'

'And our money,' put in Rose sadly. 'Eight hundred pounds we had to pay him as deposit. Bloody little creep.'

'Would the audience have to come through this room?' asked George cautiously.

'Oh, no!' said Mrs Bolitho. 'Of course your poor singers couldn't change in front of the neighbours. Imagine poor dear Poppie Pencarrow in a room full of naked young men!'

'But she'd eat them up!' laughed Rose.

'That's what I mean,' said her mother grimly. 'Even though she does have no teeth. No, we always bring them in from the other end. You'll see.' And she opened an even smaller door, hidden behind a particularly moth-eaten old tapestry. 'Look.'

George bent down. It was a remarkable sight. When 'Long Tom' Bolitho had finally, and reluctantly, sold Bolitho Hall, his three-hundred-acre sugar plantation in the parish of St James on the island of Barbados, he came back to Cornwall a very rich man.

Fashion travelling slower than gossip, most of his neighbours were still building and decorating their homes in the style of Queen Anne. 'Long Tom' was a man who liked to see how his money was spent, and to share this knowledge with those about him. Consequently he rode up to London, where a fellow sugar-planter, Thomas Dalrymple, was just putting the finishing touches to his new house in Arlington Street.

'If you'll come back to Bolitho with me, I'll see you're not the poorer for it,' he had said in his bluff way to the architect, one William Kent, who, with no other immediate prospect of employment, agreed to embark on the long and uncomfortable journey west.

The result was the gutting of the west range, until then divided between the old great hall, with the solar above another chamber at the far end. Which end that might have been was now entirely obscured, so completely was the resulting space remodelled. Purists might bewail the loss of Bolitho's medieval glories, but even George, a stranger to the study of architecture, could see the point of this room, from the massive gilded geometry of its ceiling, supported on such huge yet strangely delicate pilasters, down to the great baroque side tables with their lion faces groaning under the weight of thick kaleidoscopic marble slabs, and culminating in a titanic example, all dolphins and seahorses, which filled the great bay window looking out towards the sea.

'Will you try the piano?' It was parked in the side bay, a handsome piece of rosewood draped in some ivory lace, and covered with dusty family photographs in tarnished silver frames.

'I'd love to.' George carefully opened the lid. A Bechstein, maybe eighty to a hundred years old. He pulled up an elaborate French chair and sat gingerly on its edge. 'What do you like?'

Mother and daughter looked at each other. 'Don't you need music?' asked Rose, puzzled.

'I expect so,' he said, with a smile. 'But I'm used to busking my way through most things.'

'Well . . .' Mrs Bolitho smiled back. 'A little Chopin?' Exactly the thought Rose had had when she first saw him.

Immediately he launched into a dazzling (and

reasonably accurate) account of the 'Grande Valse Brillante', filling the tall chamber with the authentic sound of old Vienna, the Vienna of Metternich and the old order. And like the latter, he too sought variety by moving effortlessly into the great posthumous Fantaisie, sending the cascading notes soaring through the room.

Rose watched his profile, so still in contrast to the flying fingers, open-mouthed. There was a fierceness and animation about this man which she had missed, without previously identifying the loss, in the braying scrum of eligible young men she was used to. In Cornwall, these tended to be black-browed titans, given to few words, and even those laboriously mined from a vocabulary which, though rich enough in the veins of agriculture and sport, lacked depth on the world's wider issues. In London, while smaller and fairer, the ways of the 'eligible' were, if anything, less winning, since the ruling triumvirate of money, mortgage, and motor car held little power over her imagination. Indeed, her intermittent attempts at moulding potential inamorati for the better seemed only to have made matters worse. In one case much much worse. She gave an involuntary shudder. At last he stopped.

'Do you like it?' she asked him after swallowing hard. Her mother looked at her sharply.

George nodded. 'Yes,' he said quietly. 'It's excellent. Perfectly in tune.'

'Slightly unexpected in this house?' put in Mrs Bolitho, in a new tone, almost waspish.

'Where will you put the piano for the opera?' asked Rose, ignoring her.

'Over there.' He walked to the middle of the room and pointed to the centre of the wall opposite the courtyard. Suddenly he clapped his hands, twice. 'Excellent.'

'Why did you do that?' Mrs Bolitho was beginning to worry about the beef again.

'To test the acoustics. They're fine.'

'I bet you wouldn't say if they were ghastly,' whispered Rose.

George turned and stared at her, slightly put out. Then he smiled down at her. 'You're damn right,' he said. 'But this is fine. No tapestries, high ceiling, wooden floor, no problem.'

'I must go back to the kitchen,' called out Mrs Bolitho, who had suddenly identified the new note in her daughter's voice. 'Forgive me if I leave you with Rose. Lunch will be in twenty minutes.' She bustled out by the further door, which led via the Gun Room and Drawing Room back towards the kitchen. 'It could be worse,' she told herself. 'No money, of course, but that also means he won't have learnt any bad habits. And not from a family one knows, to judge by those vowels. But maybe that's a mercy too, and if the girl likes him, I think he'll do.'

'What are you muttering about?'

She nearly fell over. She'd quite forgotten about her husband, who was using the delay to polish one of his shotguns. 'Nothing, dear,' she said in a soothing voice. He would have to be kept *completely* in the dark until Rose was safely engaged. Then it would be up to Rose, and her mother had great confidence that Rose would triumph.

During lunch, which consisted of a bloody joint of beef with some watery cabbage, followed by a lemon jelly, they discussed the minutiae of the forthcoming event.

'Are you sure there's room for the orchestrah?' growled the Colonel, carefully cutting the fat off his meat.

'Daddy! You know perfectly well there's no orchestra.'

'No orchestrah! That other scoundrel never told me

that. I didn't realize *anyone* did opera without a proper orchestrah.'

'More beef, dear?' Mrs Bolitho offered her husband the dish running with scarlet scum. Rose looked as if she'd have liked to skewer him to the wall behind.

'I do believe you'll be surprised by the result,' said George tactfully.

'*Surprised?*' The Colonel let out a furious snort. 'I dare say I shall be. Yes, indeed. The most surprising thing is that we're doing it at all. We should never have agreed to carry on after your friend Boden absconded.'

George startled even himself by laughing out loud. '*Friend?* I can assure you he was no friend of mine. He was my most underhanded and deceitful rival, but he had a certain smarmy way of insinuating his way in. It's no surprise to me that he swindled you.'

The Colonel was eating hard, giving no sign of having heard. After a pause, he said, between mouthfuls, 'Could you pass the Green Label?'

'Can we just talk about bedrooms?' asked his hostess. 'I know your contract calls for a hotel. But, really, I wouldn't be happy to think of you in the Constantine Arms—'

'Mother! Really!'

'What, darling?'

'That's not a hotel. It's a . . . a dump!'

'Yes,' said her mother patiently. 'That's why I'm saying they should all stay here. Everywhere else is so far away.' A sigh of biblical proportions escaped the Colonel, now slumped back in his chair, but his wife soldiered on regardless. 'How many bedrooms would you need?'

'Well . . .' George screwed up his eyes. 'Jane and Ed would share . . .'

'Because?' The Colonel had suddenly come back to life.

'Because they're married,' said George, rather sharply. 'Then Winston and Bruno could share a twin room. That leaves four singles for Maria, Isabelle, Rupert and me.'

'Oh dear.' Mrs Bolitho had been scribbling notes. 'I've only got two other rooms, because the old service wing's got dry rot and the floorboards are all up. I don't suppose the four of you could squeeze into two? Perhaps the girls wouldn't mind sharing the big four-poster. It really is very wide. And I have got another room with two beds above the Library for you and ... er ...'

'Rupert.' George was sunk in thought. Maria and Isabelle in one bed – food indeed for thought. But him share a bedroom with Rupert? Impossible.

'Of course,' he said, seeing the older woman's woeful expression. He could not be obdurate in the face of such patent goodwill.

'Oh, I'm so glad,' she said.

George slapped his forehead. 'Oh, no! quite forgot. We must have a single room for Tim.'

'Tim?' The Colonel scented a foothold, something he could use to topple the whole *bloody* idea. He shook some sugar furiously over his jelly.

'Our tenor understudy.'

'Oh?' Rose was intrigued. 'Someone told me you didn't have understudies ...'

George grinned. 'We don't,' he said. 'Only for Rupert, our Don Ottavio.'

'Because ...?'

'Because ...' He paused. 'I shouldn't really be telling you this.'

'Do go on,' Rose said, with shining eyes.

'Well,' he said. 'Most people think understudies are there to sing in case a principal is taken ill.'

'Aren't they?'

'Oh, no!' He laughed. 'They're really just an elaborate form of psychological warfare. If Rupert has an understudy, he always performs.'

'And if not?'

'Then maybe not.'

'I can understand *that*,' said the Colonel, nodding his head vigorously. 'Makes a lot of sense. We used the same idea on the Gothic Line—'

'This Tim,' said his wife, ever adept at the pre-emptive interruption, 'is he a tenor too?'

'Oh, no!' said George. 'That would cost far too much. He's an actor, who's been resting for quite a long time. He comes for the food. But Rupert *thinks* he's a tenor, and that's more than enough.'

'He could have my room,' said Rose excitedly. 'And I could sleep on the sofa in the Library, like I did for the Hunt Ball. It was fun!' She certainly wasn't missing the chance of having George staying under the family roof.

The Colonel cleared his throat. 'I—'

'Excellent idea,' put in her mother swiftly. 'That's settled. Now I must insist that you come and see my spring border. It's never looked better, and the view of the sea is not to be missed on a day like this.'

Chapter Six

It was nearly eight o'clock when George finally parked the little Citroën on the corner of his road. Sweat was pouring down his face. Isabelle! Surely she would have gone home, furious at his leaving her on the doorstep for a whole hour, rather than welcoming her with a restoring glass of chilled Pol Roger. Or would she still be there, as smilingly eager as he? He slammed the door shut as if to punish himself for such conceited presumption, and ran down the street.

Of course, there was no one, and no message in the milk bottle either. With the final collapse of his hopes, he let himself in. Slowly and sadly, he walked straight down the corridor to his bedroom. No, there were no telephone messages either. What now? He pulled off his drenched shirt and dragged another from the drawer under his bed, wandered back to the front room and extracted a bottle of cool Beaujolais blanc. It was going to be one of those nights.

'No!' he suddenly shouted out loud. 'It wasn't my fault. Haven't you ever been late for anything?' The empty room made no reply, preserving a disapproving silence. He went across to the kitchen end of the room for the corkscrew, then traipsed back to his bedroom, threw open the window, and sat down to pull the cork. It came away in half, and as he raised the corkscrew to throw it against the wall in utter frustration, he heard the doorbell ring.

Running to the door, he flung it open. 'Isabelle!'

How had he intended to greet her? It had been the subject of much internal debate during the last twenty-four hours. A formal handshake? Too pompous. A chaste kiss on the cheek? Rather too clichéd. An arm round the waist? Much too threatening.

He needn't have worried. Her tense expression evaporated as she saw him, modulating into a wide rapturous smile, and she absolutely sprang at him, precipitating herself into his arms.

It was more than two hours later before either of them spoke another word, apart from once when, gazing up at him in the heat of their struggle, she had suddenly cried, '*Éventrez-moi!*' And then again, louder, '*Éventrez-moi!*'

'I really needed that.' She was lying on her back, smiling at the ceiling. George tried to speak, and ended by just nodding. She turned her face towards him. 'Did I please you?'

Pulling himself awkwardly up on one elbow, he leant over and kissed her breasts. 'Yes,' he croaked. 'You know you did.' She smelt delicious.

Isabelle laughed delightedly. 'I'll please you some more in a minute.' Poor George! He managed a smile. 'Is there anything to drink?'

'I've got a bottle of Beaujolais blanc somewhere, but the cork's stuck.'

'Hand it over, *chéri*. I will show you how to deal with recalcitrant corks, and then . . .' She licked her swollen lips.

'And then?' he said nervously.

With good reason, for she suddenly vaulted on top

of him, grabbing his wrists and pinning them down on the rumpled sheet. 'Turn over, Georges, and I will show you a little trick that may surprise you.'

'Well? Did that surprise you?' George stared at her, speechless. Yet there was something in his expression that evidently pleased her, for she leant down and kissed him tenderly on both his eyes. 'Let's get some sleep. Then you can drive me home, as I have to do an audition at eleven.'

'An audition?' He sat up abruptly. 'Who for?'

She laughed delightedly. 'I thought that might bring you back to life! You impresarios! You're all the same. Don't disquiet yourself, *chéri*. It is only for a concert in the autumn. We will spend the whole summer like this, singing and fucking. Will that please you?' He grinned, and nodded. Within three minutes, they were both asleep.

In another room, in another part of the sleeping city, a figure was bent over a desk, carefully cutting letters, words, and sometimes even whole phrases out of a pile of old newspapers. To one side were some discarded newspapers with small square and rectangular holes evident among the crumpled pages. To the other was a stout pot of glue, with obscene pink lips, slanted like a pig's snout. From time to time the figure up-ended the pot, and drew its lips across the single sheet of typing paper, so that they were forced open, dribbling a thin smear of greyish glue which shone in the oblique light thrown by an angle-poise lamp. To this viscous surface the tiny off-cuts were then carefully applied. The room stank of sweat and glue.

At last the figure sat back with a contented sigh,

held up the paper with hands encased in transparent plastic medical gloves, and re-read it carefully before folding and placing it in an already prepared envelope. Satisfaction comes to all in many guises, but there was a marked difference between the blissful expressions on the faces of those two happy sleepers in Hammersmith, compared to the grotesque contortion on the face of this other.

Chapter Seven

'Listen.' Bruno, dagger in hand, was very pink in the face. 'I repeat, as for the brain-dead. I am saying: "Yes, I will fight with you, if you wish to die." *If you wish to die!* How can I say that as if sharing a joke with him? And, more to the point, is it *likely* he would come up and hug me, for Christ's sake?'

Jane Nuneham smiled patiently. 'I hear what you're saying, Bruno. Let's sit down for a moment and I'll explain it again.' She flashed a look at the mighty Winston, who was peering at them from out of a large laundry basket. He winked back and she felt an emptiness in the pit of her stomach, a void she urgently wanted him to fill.

'What's happening?' called George anxiously from the piano, where he was going through the list of musical cuts with old Mr Sumption, employed as *répétiteur* for a knockdown hundred pounds for the week and a credit in the programme.

Nearer, uncomfortably so, was her husband Ed, clutching a massive two-handed broadsword in the first part of his double act as the old Commendatore before a quick change turned him into the younger, though equally unfortunate, Masetto. He had seen her glance, and the wink, and recognized the reaction. By God, he was thinking, if that black bastard thinks he's got a chance of getting into her knickers, he'd better watch out for me. The trouble was . . . Jane! As he had learnt when they first met, although then her enthusiasm for the joys of nature had operated in his favour. But now . . . he had the sword!

'Just explaining the motivation,' called back Jane.

George glowered. 'Try saying we've got this room for six hours' rehearsal a day for six days, that's thirty-six hours, and you've had nearly two hours already. You're only on page seventeen, and you've still got another two hundred and eighty-nine to go!'

'Look,' said Jane, turning back to Bruno. 'Everyone does it that the old man challenges him, they fight and he kills the old fool.' This with a wintry look at her fuming husband.

'Yes,' said Bruno. 'That's because that's how it's written.'

'Fine, but we want these people to remember us, particularly those who've seen it a hundred times. We want to encourage these people to employ us again. I've read the background plays. Did you know that in the earliest Spanish play, Don Giovanni's father and the Commendatore were best friends?'

Bruno shrugged sulkily. 'No. So what?'

'So, is it likely the Don would be running in and out of women's bedrooms with some claymore clanking about and getting in the way between his legs?'

'It's possible.'

'Isn't it more likely, when raping his next-door neighbour, that he'd disguise himself and carry a small dagger instead of a hulking great broadsword? You haven't seen it yet, but you're going to be wearing a really sinister black silk mask.'

'Oh?' Bruno liked black silk. He always felt good in silk, and people told him he looked good in black. *'Really?'*

'Yes. So when the old moron surprises you, blundering about with his massive weapon . . .'

'Truly?' This as an aside from Winston, just loud enough for Jane to hear, not loud enough for Ed to be sure.

She giggled, then straightened her face. 'As I say, he's got the drop on you. But you play it's like a charade. It's a joke. He pulls off your mask. Hey! It's my old pal Don G. He relaxes. He laughs. He goes to hug you, 'cos he's very very relieved. Out comes the retractable knife from behind your back, and you stick it into the condom full of stage blood which we'll attach to Ed's leather guard under his night-shirt. And there you have a bit of a show-stopper, right? At least I'm not asking you to do it in the nude with oxy-acetylene torches, or setting the show in a Brooklyn abattoir.'

'I think your idea's *great*,' shouted out Winston. 'Really great.'

'Thank you,' said Jane, ignoring a contemptuous snort from her husband. 'Bruno?'

Bruno was frowning. 'But if I'm wearing a mask,' he said slowly, 'the audience won't see my face.'

Jane closed her eyes momentarily. 'You're only wearing it for half the first scene – what, forty bars?'

'A hundred and one,' called out Mr Sumption in a quavery voice.

'Well, a hundred and one then,' snapped Jane. 'But think of the impact!'

Bruno was stroking his chin. 'I'm not sure I see the Don as quite such a shit.'

'Oh, great!' shouted Winston, emerging from the laundry basket. 'The first man to play Don Giovanni in the style of Jimmy Stewart. Why don't you go the whole hog and do him as Dick Van Dyke?'

Bruno was frowning again. 'On the other hand . . .'

'What?'

'If it was a *violet* silk mask . . .'

'It's going to be black,' said George, in a very quiet voice. He had walked over to join them. 'And you're going to do it Jane's way, or you leave the rehearsals now. She's directing, you're singing. But if you do leave, I'll go straight to court and get judgment for that hundred pound advance and put it in the hands of the most impatient and *violent* debt collector I know. Your choice. It's a shame because I think you'd make a stupendous Don. You've got a fabulous voice, the women will really go for you, the men too, and any critic—'

'OK! OK! I hear you.' Bruno held up his hands in mock surrender. He turned to Jane and showed her his teeth. 'You're the boss. Let's get this show on the road.'

'Well, *really!*' Watching this scene, with his feet up on the piano, was a long, lanky man with crinkly fair hair and large floppy hands with nails cut perfectly straight. His eyes were rather close together on either side of a long pointed nose, and his mouth, which undulated rather more than was normal, was turned down in an expression of disgust. 'You did lay that on thick. And I mean thick.'

George allowed himself a tight little smile. 'Think, Rupert. Where would I get someone else now? We're ten days away from the first show.'

'And what,' asked the fair man, widening his eyes provocatively, 'will you be doing to terrorize poor little me into doing your will?'

'Nothing,' said George succinctly. He leant forward and patted the tenor's cheek. 'I'd put Tino Tragliava on instead.'

'Tragliava! That little turd!'

'Oh, come,' said George. 'He's got a fine voice, though not,' he added hastily, 'as fine as yours.' It didn't do to push Rupert Brock too far, as he had a tendency to convert a barely manageable drink problem into several weeks' hospitalization.

'Why isn't he here rehearsing?'

'Oh . . .' George waved his hands vaguely. 'He's been talked through the production. He's got the gist. You know we can't really afford understudies. It's only because he *loves* this part so. He'd kill to perform it. But I'm counting on you to save me the extra money.' He made a mental note to remind Tim about this extra motivation in his role as the tenor-in-waiting.

'You said he felt the same thing about Ferrando when we were doing *Così*,' said Rupert suspiciously.

George nodded. 'I think it's just he's got a thing about you, Rupert. He knows everyone thinks you're better, and he desperately wants to make them reconsider.'

'Well, he won't get the chance, matey,' said Rupert, with sudden conviction. 'I've never let you down yet. Jesus! When are they going to get to my first scene?'

'Coming up!' shouted Jane, who had heard this last exchange during a lull in the music. 'Get into position with Maria. Door Two, remember?'

Maria herself had spent the second hour glowering at George from a chair placed firmly in the opposite corner, having adroitly missed the first hour by the simple expedient of arriving late.

'Dear Jane,' she had said on arriving. 'You are so thorough. I knew you would still be in the overture.'

'Well, we aren't,' had been the angry reply. 'We've wasted forty minutes waiting for you.'

'I hope you were practising your aria, dear,' said Maria. 'I know the trouble it gives you.'

'But we've cut "Mi tradi",' said George without thinking.

'Now, I do call that *very wise*, Giorgio, *caro*,' the prima donna had replied with a triumphant smile. '*Very wise indeed*.'

After that, Jane had not looked at her once, addressing her stage directions for Donna Anna as if to some disembodied spirit hovering over her enemy's substantial bulk. Isabelle, as Zerlina, was not due until after lunch, which she and George had agreed to take together at the little bistro just down the street.

Chapter Eight

He could hardly be said to be in love with her. How could he be, when they had gone straight from first sight to fixated lovers without the benefit of a single conversation?

Respect. Friendship. Shared humour quotient. How could they assess these, when they only knew how to make love to each other? Yet his thoughts were only, and always, of her.

She had moved a few things over from her flat in Bayswater and they had spent every moment of free time among those scarlet sheets. So much so that she had never even seen his living room. Their one weekend they had driven north to a country-house hotel, to combine good food with a sturdy four-poster.

Now that rehearsals were getting under way, with people calling on him unexpectedly and at all hours, he had agreed to do a swap, and spend the next few weeks at her address, to avoid damaging morale by making their mutual infatuation too obvious. There is always enough jealousy among singers anyway, without confusing the group emotions further by revealing that the musical director was already bedding the soubrette.

The afternoon rehearsals went smoothly, so much so that they were well into her duet with Bruno by the time Jane called out: 'Five-thirty! That's it, folks. Ten-thirty tomorrow, and don't forget to bring your own tea-bags. This isn't the YMCA! And ten-thirty means ten-thirty start work, not ten-thirty meander in and start making coffee. Right?'

Isabelle hurried out, refusing Bruno's offer of a lift, and ran round the corner to wait just beyond the bus stop. George stayed behind until Ed, as stage-manager, had locked up the hall. He then drove nonchalantly towards the river before suddenly doing a U-turn and nipping round the new housing estate, emerging to pick up Isabelle just as, unobserved by either of them, Rupert emerged from the newsagent opposite.

'I love you.'

'I love you.' They paused to kiss lingeringly, unself-consciously, and then he drove her back through Earl's Court, following her directions through Kensington and Holland Park until at last she indicated a tall white stucco building beside a chunky brown church. 'Here we are. Park there.'

'Don't I need a resident's permit?'

'You can worry about that in an hour's time.'

'An hour . . .?'

'Come on!' She grabbed his hand and pulled him into the building and up the stairs. At the fourth floor, with both of them short of breath, she took out some keys and let him through a tall green door and into a corridor that smelt deliciously of fresh flowers.

'This is lovely, Isabelle.' Already she was pressing against him, one supple leg raised as if to encircle his waist. There was a big poster of blood-red poppies opposite, and a watercolour of Chartres over a small table dominated by a vase of lilies.

'This way.' She led him into a little living room, with severe French furniture covered in green velvet and a gilt and glass dining table at one end. Something in his manner alarmed her. 'Don't you like it, *chéri*?' she asked, suddenly anxious.

He didn't reply. He was staring at an eight-foot-high blue and white glazed Viennese rococo stove.

'What is it? What's the matter?' She ran at him, pulling him as tight to her as she could. 'Please tell me. Please.'

He shook his head angrily, confused by the sudden surge of jealous rage that had overwhelmed him. Isabelle. With Szelko! His *father*! Who must now be nearly ninety. 'How *could* you?' He hadn't meant to speak, and certainly not in such a vindictive tone. But the inner compulsion was too great. 'Where did you meet him?'

'What are you talking about?' She was staring at him, confused, but also with defensive anger rising at his hostile tone.

'That! That badge of surrender!' Yet if he felt like that, why had he kept his mother's with such proprietary pride?

'That? The stove?' She laughed aloud, though still with a puzzled air. 'That was my mother's. It was a wedding present. From an old admirer.'

'A wedding present?' The back of his head was tingling, as if at the start of a bout of flu. 'To your mother?'

She nodded cheerfully. 'Yes. I have a picture of her somewhere. She sang Sophie at the Festival de Toulouse. It was her last part before they married. My father was in the chorus. That's how they met. Romantic, no?'

'And who was conducting?' said George slowly, although he already knew the answer.

'Oskar Szelko, the Austrian conductor. In fact,' her blue eyes sparkled, their gold flecks reflecting her sense of delicious complicity, 'I will let you into a little secret. Szelko—'

'I know,' he said, his voice heavy with despair, 'he was your father. As he was mine. Oh, Isabelle.' She was shocked to see tears spilling down his face unchecked. 'You're my *sister*!'

52

'Really?' She laughed all the more. 'You say half-sister, don't you? That doesn't count. We must celebrate.' And she took his hand.

'But, Isabelle ...'

'Do I have to beg?' She was on her knees now, worrying at him and looking up with such a beguiling smile, her inimitable look of droll expectancy. The worst of it was, he wanted her even more.

'This is wrong!'

'Ah, *chéri*, so much is wrong in this life.' She kissed his hand. 'And a little gossip? Who knows the truth?'

'We do.' And yet he was already half out of his clothes.

'Perhaps. Perhaps we are wrong.'

'But if we are right?' One shoelace had knotted.

'*Oh, chéri!* If we're right, we're wrong. And if we're wrong, then we're right. *C'est parfait!*' She laughed delightedly. 'Now, hush! I need your full attention.'

There was silence, or nearly silence, in the room until she was able to sigh contentedly. 'There ... I knew you'd see it my way! Oh!' Her smile was positively seraphic. '*Que j'adore mon frère!*'

Chapter Nine

Don't think you haven't been spotted, fucking that girl whose young enough to be your daughter. Not that she's ANY BETTER, shagging that black bastard behind your back.

A Friend.

George stared at the flimsy sheet, stiffened in places by the cut-out letters glued to the thin blue airmail paper. Isabelle. With Winston! His mind momentarily lost focus in giving way to a furious and miserable picturing of the scene. How could she give that exquisite body to that . . .? And yet he liked Winston, and knew it even as he raged against him with unconsidered venom. He put the letter down and, suddenly, almost taking himself by surprise, he chuckled. 'At least the bastard doesn't know she's my *sister*!'

But who on earth could have sent him such a malicious letter? Wasn't the poison pen supposed to be the prerogative of women? Jane? Maria?

Maria! Yet it didn't sound, or feel, like her. Maria, for all her faults, could never be jealous, being so imperishably convinced of her own superiority. Yet she was a singer! And singers, by definition, were creatures of chaos, and for a good reason: businessmen can check their letters, cameramen can re-examine their films, but a singer can only rely on others for a judgement on her stock-in-trade, that is, her voice. And those others may be so unreliable. Her singing-teacher? Only anxious to retain the weekly fee. Her colleagues? Jealous and just as insecure themselves. The audience? What do they know, when most of them are half-asleep!

He read the letter again, tore it in half and scrumpled it into a tiny ball before throwing it into the raffia basket behind the sofa. Filth! And yet why shouldn't she? Isabelle was a normal healthy female. If her brother wouldn't sleep with her – and he wouldn't, hadn't indeed for the last four days since discovering their predicament – then why shouldn't she seek sexual quietus from another? Like Winston. He swore loudly, and kicked the stove. So soon? Deep inside the stove, a thin ceramic note of protest reverberated around its serpentine belly. His natural father had a lot to answer for. 'You bastard!' he shouted suddenly. 'You only ever thought of yourself! Damn you! Damn you to hell!'

The rehearsals were almost complete, with their first performance on the approaching Friday. When he arrived, quite late, at the hall, Jane had set up a table with a single massive candelabrum holding a dozen or so tall candles beside which Bruno, in a hired costume splendidly be-sequined, was miming the dismemberment of a cooked chicken with his bare hands.

'This looks promising.'

'Wait till you see the bill for that effing candlestick,' muttered Ed, whose temper had deteriorated during a week spent juggling two roles as well as stage-managing the show and trying to protect his wife's chastity – no easy job, especially when she showed no sign of welcoming his vigil.

'It's only hired, isn't it?' asked George anxiously. He

could see, but was trying to ignore, Isabelle's provocative blue gaze from her chair beside Mr Sumption.

'You'll be buying it if that clown drops it again.'

'*L'ultima prova*...' It was Jane, as Donna Elvira, coming to interrupt the Don's feast. She swept up to the table, and started an Italianate row with her stage partner, gloriously Mozartian in its rollicking beauty.

'*Vivan le femine! Viva il buon vino!*' Bruno was toasting her ironically, with Winston behind him ready to pour more wine, and laughing at his master's cruel effrontery. Suddenly Jane seized the tablecloth and, just as Bruno whisked away his plate and Winston grabbed the heavy candelabrum, she swept the cloth aside, whereupon they both replaced the plate and candlestick in a single swift movement. It was slick, and impressive.

'Great! Brilliant!' George was laughing at the smoothness of the operation. 'It's the super-quick timing of the *re*placing that makes it funny.'

Jane gave him a withering look. 'So glad you're pleased,' she said. 'We've spent over an hour getting it right.'

'Careful with that,' said George suddenly, seeing the candles wobble in their holders.

'You try holding it!' snapped Jane. 'Winston's doing a great job.'

'Winston! *Winston!* WINSTON! That's all you ever say.' There was a shattering crash as Bruno hurled his glass, the chicken and its plate across the stone floor. 'How can I eat a bloody bird *and* sing *and* hold this glass with you waving your hormones about like a fucking washing line?'

'What glass?' murmured Rupert, looking across at the shattered remnants.

'Oh! *Oh!*' Jane was facing one way, then the other, her face flooded with an angry flush. '*Oh!*' She burst into noisy sobs and ran out of the room.

'Oh, *Giorgio*.' Maria had a grin slashed right across her face. 'I knew how it would be if you had Jane back. But you wouldn't listen to your Maria.'

Ed, who had been silently sweeping up the wreckage, stood up, his face as white as Jane's had been dark. He walked over to Maria. 'You bitch!' His chest was heaving and one hand was curled into a fist the size of a prize cauliflower.

To everyone's amazement, Maria let out a gurgle of carefree laughter. Then she tapped him on the nose with her right forefinger. 'Now, *Edmundo, caro*! This is no way to speak to your old friend Maria. You must save your voice for Saturday.'

He nodded. 'You're right.' And returned quietly to the debris. She began to laugh out loud.

'Maria . . .' George could feel his own anger getting the better of him.

'Go to Jane!' she snapped. 'Another two minutes of this caterwauling and she won't even manage the ensembles on Saturday. For all our sakes, shut her up!' And as he obeyed her too, George was very conscious of her professionalism, and Ed's, which could always be relied upon to overcome any unscheduled outbreaks of temperament. Maria was an opera singer first, and an impossibly infuriating diva second. It was that crucial order of priorities which kept her in work.

Poor George! Abruptly deprived (by his own scruples) of that most soothing of all physical balms, the loving attention of a beautiful woman – albeit in this case his sister – he was reduced to asking himself several times that day how he had ever got into such an emotionally over-charged business.

It was not just that his work required him to watch this sister–lover coiling herself round a variety of men each day in rehearsals as part of *her* work, nor even that he was himself supposed to be playing an exceptionally demanding score while thus being tortured. It was also that he had to minister to all the other emotional imbroglios of a closely knit company of sexually active adults, without allowing his own sorrows to distract him or, worse, become public. Maria probably guessed, she was forever giving him long soupy stares overflowing with a sticky mixture of forgiveness and desire. And the poison-pen merchant, too.

That evening, with the complicated chorus of the opera's finale safely rehearsed (including Ed's lightning change from avengingly statuesque Commendatore back to peasant-boy Masetto) until they were all exhausted by its repetition, George released them. Walking out into the fading light, he decided to take the District Line Underground across town to St James's Park for a wine tasting at Christie's. Since Winston lived south of the river, they travelled together as far as Victoria, but George's intention of some discreet questioning about Isabelle was forestalled on the platform by Winston's taking out a neat black pocket tape-recorder.

'Catching up on the music?' asked George with what he hoped was a friendly smile.

'Meditation,' was the reply. 'Helps a lot.'

'Can I listen?'

The big man handed the earphones without answering. George put them on. 'Ommm,' said a voice on the tape. 'We will all say: "Ommmm", now. Ommmm.' George saw Winston was watching him and smiled. 'Now we will all say: "Ommm",' intoned the voice. 'Ommmmm.' Someone was jogging his elbow. He opened his eyes. It was Winston mouthing something. 'What?'

'The train's in. Come on.'

There were only two empty seats, on opposite sides, so George sat looking around at his fellow-passengers, while Winston, with a young blonde woman on one side of him and an older brunette clutching a briefcase on the other, settled his headphones into position. Both women were staring into space.

Could Winston really have moved in on Isabelle already? Had she nothing to get over, no feelings for . . .? Stations came and went.

He looked up. Something had happened. The women on either side of Winston were both still staring straight ahead of them, but with strained taut faces. The blonde had clenched her fists so tight that her knuckles were white. He could hardly hear himself think above the rattle of the train. The coach was swaying and – it happened again. Both women flinched and their eyes seemed momentarily to flicker sideways. Had it been his imagination or had Winston's lips moved? He leant forward.

'Ommm,' said Winston, quite loudly. The blonde woman had suddenly acquired an obsessive interest in whatever advertisement was pasted above George's head. She stared at it with rabid concentration, as if it held the key to the secrets of the universe.

'Ommm,' Winston said again, louder. The brunette buried her head in her book, which she seemed now to grasp as one might a potential weapon. The blonde, her eyes still fixed sightlessly on the advertisement, had blushed a painful crimson, the colour starting in the veins of her cheeks and nose, and spreading slowly outwards until her whole face burned with colour. And then, salvation! Bright lights, deceleration, a crowded station, Victoria already, and they watched Winston's burly shape retreating among the disembarking crowd. The two women settled back into their seats with evident relief, rolling their eyes at each other in the momentary communion of fellow-sufferers. George waited until the train was back on the move before he was unable to resist leaning forward in a confiding way and whispering a conspiratorial 'Ommmm!'

Chapter Ten

A storm was building up off Bolitho Head. Thick salty gusts, laden with spray, were whipping the Atlantic into a frenzy of almost sexual frustration, with its waves pounding and pounding again against the pent-up rocks below the house. The air was thick too, hot and humid, under a lowering sky which filtered the watery light to an atmospheric blue, so that even the trees seemed to wilt and change shape before the threatened outburst.

The house had prepared itself with its accustomed phlegm, crouching stonily among the rhododendrons, its low windows like eyes half-closed against an onslaught. A thousand such storms had broken against its heavy grey slates, and no doubt a thousand more would make as little lasting impact.

Nor was the atmosphere inside the house less over-wrought. Of the hundred and thirty white and gold chairs to be positioned in the Saloon on the night, only seventy would hold that essential commodity of show business: a bottom whose owner had paid for its seat. Sixty-seven friends and neighbours had duly sent their cheques for sixty pounds each. With George's fee of over four thousand pounds including tax, plus the first lost deposit of nine hundred pounds to his fugitive competitor, and the hire of the chairs from Exeter, there was still an embarrassing shortfall in place of the two or three thousand pounds they had hoped to raise for Rose's hospice.

As purple as the approaching storm's light upon her first summer roses, so purple also was her husband's nose among the warmer shade of his cheeks as Mary Bolitho explained the arithmetic of the coming invasion of his home's precious peace.

'You mean,' he was beginning to breathe very noisily, ' – that this *opera* – ' and there was something in the way he said it which gave it an almost lavatorial contempt '– will actually lose us *a thousand pounds*?'

'More or less.'

'More or less! Good God, woman . . .'

She smiled at him. Let no one underestimate Mary Bolitho's tactics. The Colonel might have – did, indeed – lead the fabled tank charge at Schulenberg which prompted the incredulous German commander to quote Schiller among the burning ruins of his meticulously prepared defences: *'Mit der Dummheit kämpfen die Götter selbst vergebens!'* And if the great dramatist was correct, that against stupidity even the gods battle in vain, how much vainer were the Colonel's defences against his wily wife.

For in that smile lay the distilled essence of thirty years of marital nurture. Had she not soothed his fevers in the hill stations of the Punjab, and warmed his aching flanks on those long cold desert nights when the Carthaginian sand around them lay as white and unforgiving as marble? More to the point, had she not battled year after year with Mrs Tregeare over the latter's habit of undercooking his breakfast bacon? His anger melted away before the warm memories implicit in that smile and, with the solitary rebellion of a little sigh, he drew out his pipe and settled back to a silent communion with his one companion who never answered back: the faithful, unchanging and sympathetic *Daily Telegraph*.

'*Dad!*'

'Eh? . . . What?'

'I've done it!' Rose had burst into the room. 'You know those new people who bought Tredinnick?'

'Damned city slickers!'

'That's them. He's called Clay Hammerson.'

'He would be.'

'He's going to sponsor the evening.'

'What's the catch?'

'There is no catch. He's putting up five thousand pounds for thirty front row seats and a room here to entertain some corporate colleagues. Every penny raised by ticket sales will go straight to the charities!'

The Colonel had always wondered how it would feel for iron to enter his soul. Now he knew. It wasn't a gradual intrusion, tactfully camouflaged. It was a sudden and savage insertion of rusted metal, grinding promiscuously into his vitals.

'Corporate colleagues?' he cried. 'In *Bolitho*?'

'Dad! Five thousand smackers!'

He paused. It was a remarkable sum. 'I suppose,' he mused, 'we could let him have the old Billiards Room?' Yes, the pass had been sold. Farewell the purity of the Colonel's soul! Farewell the inviolate privacy of Bolitho Court! Pounds sterling had won over pride of place and race.

'With all the wallpaper falling off?' shrieked Rose.

'Certainly not! I told him he could have this room.' After that the Colonel took his newspaper upstairs.

What they none of them knew down in Cornwall was that the reason for this sudden munificence lay with the Floria Tosca Grand Opera Company's first performance the week before. The dress rehearsal had passed off tolerably well, apart from Maria losing her way twice in her main aria and Rupert missing out a large chunk of

63

his part of the 'Prayer' trio, causing a corresponding confusion among George at the piano and Maria and Jane on stage.

Their first engagement was at Almondsbury House, seat of Lord Harrogate, a middle-aged Hertfordshire magnate whose interest in the arts extended no further than the occasional assignation with junior members of the Covent Garden *corps de ballet*. Lady Harrogate, however, a dumpy cheerful soul, only too grateful to be spared her husband's increasingly bizarre attentions at night, opened her doors once a year in aid of the Hertfordshire Fund for the Protection of Endangered Species. But both husband and wife were alike in one respect. The difference between one opera company and another was to both of them as indistinct as that between two garages on the Great North Road.

'Here we are.' At three o'clock, Ed drove the van up to the front of the long façade and parked by some artistically curving steps. Mistaking his hostess, who was waiting to welcome him at the front door, for a maid, he handed her the boot-bag and marched into the hall. 'Any sign of the Wotsits?'

She gave him a tight little smile. 'I'm Sylvia Harrogate,' she said, staggering slightly under the weight of the bag. 'Perhaps I can help.'

'Oh?' This was not the sort of situation that found Ed at his best. 'Can we talk about the cast's meal?'

'If we must.' She put the bag down as gently as she could and led him into her boudoir, a tall room with eau-de-nil walls and a painted ceiling showing nymphs and shepherds in frolicsome mood. 'I have a note from Mr ... er ... Sinclair to say you will be nine in number and will be eating at six.'

'Five-thirty,' corrected Ed. 'We take two hours to digest.'

'Very well.' She made a note on George's letter. 'I

can easily change that. Mrs Chambers will show you where to go in due course.'

'We have three vegetarians.' He had spotted the ceiling, and was craning his head round to follow one particularly adventurous nymph.

'Indeed?'

'Yes.' Ed forced himself to concentrate on the dumpy old bag in front of him rather than the gorgeous creature above. 'Did he mention about hot soup?'

'No,' she said. 'He didn't.'

'That's vital,' said Ed, aware that his dress, torn blue jeans and a string vest, were increasingly the subject of disdainful scrutiny.

'Don't forget Bruno,' said Winston, putting his head round the door. 'He's a vegan now. Hello.' He smiled at Lady Harrogate. 'Nice place you've got here.'

'And he's allergic to *cheese*,' shouted Jane from the hall.

'Well,' said Lady Harrogate, standing up. 'I've enjoyed our little chat. There'll be shepherd's pie and fruit salad in the nursery at five-thirty. If anybody wants anything else, I believe there's one of those Tesco shops in Watford.' She made it sound like a public lavatory.

'Buggering old bitch,' muttered Ed to Winston after the chatelaine had withdrawn upstairs. 'Doesn't she realize what a strain we're under?' Nor was Lady Harrogate's own enraged report to her husband, upstairs in his office, any the less pungent.

By five the troupe was in undisputed possession of the Almondsbury House ballroom, a huge square of a room, hung with faded blue and grey tapestries and lit by two swirling wooden chandeliers poised above their heads like massive tarantulas ready to strike.

'Shall we run the finale?' George, seated at the piano,

was trying to ignore the tension among his cast. Ed, his stomach bulging through that awful string vest, was glaring at Jane, who was laughing loudly with Winston; Bruno was casting languishing looks at a silent withdrawn Isabelle; Maria was doing the same to George himself; and Rupert was glowering at the tenth, and newest, member of the group, a squat expressionless older man seated beside George. This was Tim, alias Tino Tragliava, the silent 'tenor', a man whose run of resting from theatrical employment was now into its sixth sensational year. A friend of George's since shared days at the Dollis Hill Polytechnic, Tim was only too pleased to play the, so far, undemanding role of page-turner-cum-tenor-in-waiting in return for a square meal and occasional cash.

'You're still the same devious bastard,' he muttered to George, turning the page of the score for the final scene.

'Just as well,' whispered George, 'with this lot to control.'

'You can say that again. Bunch of raving loonies, as per usual. I can't believe you've still got that crazy Maria in the cast.'

'She's got a fine voice.'

'You used to be more interested lower down,' murmured Tim, with an oddly humourless wink. 'But, then, singers are all alike, aren't they?'

George stared at him. There was no doubt that Tim was beginning to look older. The skin round his nose was blotched and there were deepening lines below his eyes and on either side of his fleshy mouth. 'What do you mean?'

'Stick it in! Pull 'em out and wave 'em in your face. That's all they ever think about, isn't it?' Tim wiped his mouth on the back of his sleeve.

'Are actors so different?' George had begun to play the music for the next recit.

66

Tim shook his head, and turned away to watch Bruno's entrance. He muttered something, but so quietly that George couldn't hear.

Despite their various dietary disciplines, everyone tucked into the shepherd's pie with zeal, and, even more surprising, the first act went perfectly.

In the interval, Lord Harrogate poked his head round the door of what was normally his office but which for this one night had become the opera changing room. It being a warm night, Bruno and Rupert were stripped to their briefs, and Maria wore only the scantiest of underclothes, but their host's poise never wavered. 'Um ... Mr Sinclair?'

George, who had been checking a cut in the score with Tim, hurried over. 'Yes, Lord Harrogate?'

'Could we have a word?'

George followed him out and firmly closed the door behind him. 'Yes?'

'We're all enormously enjoying the show.'

'Thank you very much.'

'Your Donna ... um ... Anna. She's frightfully good.' Something in the way he said this caused George to look at his employer more closely. He was plump, with a smooth, well-cared-for complexion and pale eyes set rather close together. But there was something about his lower lip, its fullness perhaps, or even its slight droop, which gave him a definite air of instability. 'Someone, I can't remember who, said she was ... er ... your *friend*.'

What business was it of this fat moron? For an instant George was on the verge of losing his temper. But then he remembered that this was a fat moron wearing a dinner jacket in whose pocket might be resting an envelope containing a large cheque made out in the name of George Sinclair. Such a treasure trail was not lightly to be ignited.

Instead of George the Offended Gentleman, then, it had to be George the Man of the World. He dredged up a conspiratorial twinkle, no mean feat.

'No longer,' he said.

'Ah.' Lord Harrogate's gaze slithered away and focused on some object in the far distance. 'Is she . . . er . . .?'

'Is she . . .?' George could hear Ed ringing the bell to summon the audience back for Act Two.

'Is she . . . er . . .' Would the man never spit it out? ' . . . um . . . is she *strict*?'

How on earth should he answer that one? 'No, she's never tied me up with barbed wire and flogged my extremities'? Or, 'Yes, she'll do anything you ask once you've got her enzymes heaving'? George stared at the beleaguered peer, so ill at ease on his own ancestral floorboards. 'I think,' he said judiciously, 'it might be better to ask her that yourself.' And managed another smile.

'Thank you so much.' Lord Harrogate's eyes managed a momentary contact, their pupils looming large and black. 'Perhaps after the show? Some champagne in the Drawing Room for you and her . . . oh . . . and the little blonde girl. I've got a business friend staying who'd very much like to meet her. Which is rather brave of him in the circumstances.'

'It's very difficult to separate the cast,' said George truthfully.

'Just see what you can do, there's a good fellow.' Lord Harrogate had unbent as far as he could. 'I don't think the others . . . my wife . . . er . . . it's tricky.'

'I'll do what I can,' said George. Realistically, he doubted if even champagne would lure anyone into close proximity with the Harrogates.

In fact it all went as smoothly as the second act. Maria hit her top notes with thrilling accuracy, Ed dragged

Bruno off to 'hell' (alias the Billiards Room) through dense clouds of smoke noisily unleashed by Jane, still in her costume as Donna Elvira behind the Ballroom door, and when, after a storm of clapping, George went back to the changing room, where he could see a queue of women clamouring to be introduced to Bruno, he met Isabelle and Maria coming the other way, just the two of them, apparently now on the friendliest of terms, both laughing about Maria's wig coming momentarily adrift in her last aria. It was, indeed, one of the phenomena of each year's tour, that just as the unlikeliest couple would end up inextricably entwined, so equally improbable people became friends and allies.

'Now,' he said to them abruptly. 'You've both been invited for champagne in the Drawing Room, wherever that is.'

'All of us?' enquired Maria, impressed.

'No,' said George. 'Just you two. So please don't say anything. Go if you'd like to, but don't upset Rupert.'

'Rupert *loves* a lord,' said Maria archly.

'Well, it could be your turn,' said George.

'Should we give you a percentage?' Isabelle was glowering at him.

'Suit yourself,' he snapped. 'I didn't ask you to flirt so outrageously with that man in the white tuxedo. Who ever heard of Zerlina sitting on somebody's lap in the middle of her aria? *That* wasn't in the production.'

'Nor was the note you played anything to do with Mozart's score!' she snapped back. 'Anyway, they laughed, didn't they?'

'Come on,' said Maria, grabbing her hand, excited. 'If he's willing to sell our bodies, let's not lose out on the champagne. It's his loss, and our gain.' Suddenly they both started laughing. George turned away angrily and hurried down the corridor. Bruno, in a black and yellow striped dressing-gown, was flirting with one of the prettier women, while the others looked on.

Inside the changing room, Ed, very white in the face, was throwing the boots back into their faded canvas bag, while Rupert and Tim sat ignoring each other at opposite ends of the room.

'Where's the lavatory?' said George.

'Past that room they call the pantry,' called out Tim, after Ed had ignored the question altogether.

'I'll find it.' There was a burst of loud laughter outside.

Beyond the butler's pantry there were doors everywhere, doors to cupboards, doors to housemaid's closets, doors to . . . He stopped dead. The door he had opened had precipitated him onto a tableau of such startling and disturbing beauty that he was held mesmerized by its power. The plain truth, immediately apparent, was that Jane was lying on some sort of rug being energetically penetrated by Winston. But there was nothing plain about this truth. Her skin shone in the shadows like the purest white marble, here a leg, there a breast, with her head flung back taut in the ecstasy of rococo fulfilment. In the deepest and richest contrast, Winston's long back was that of a Baroque satyr, rough-hewn from gleaming ebony and lit by a thousand infinitesimal beads of sparkling sweat, his muscles undulating the rich texture of his skin with the violence of his efforts. And even as George stood there, his own chest heaving with the emotions aroused, a slender white arm, as mystic, as wonderful in that light as was ever raised from any lake, snaked round, each ivory finger tensed with separate serpentine intent. Slithering between those dripping buttocks, they precipitated a final Herculean heave when the two sculptures, so contrasted in their extremes of light and shade, seemed to coalesce, to meld tenderly together, changing from Gods to humans again, from Nature back to nature, with one deep harmonious and exhausted sigh.

It was only as he turned away, ashamed to have witnessed so private and, despite the violence, so intensely moving a scene, that he came face to face with Ed himself.

'Ah!' Swiftly he grabbed the big man's arm. 'Quick! Can you give me a hand loading the costumes.'

'*Out of my way!*' Ed pushed George aside so hard that he jarred his shoulder against the closet door. '*Where's my wife?*' Silence followed, and then Ed walked slowly back into the light of the corridor. 'Loading some costumes?' he said quietly. 'Let's get on with it.'

'Right.' George knew better than to contradict him. 'Over here.'

For half an hour they meticulously folded and packed the costumes in layers of tissue paper and laid them in the two laundry baskets. And all the time, tears, unchecked, rolled down the big man's fiery cheeks. Yet he never spoke a word.

Chapter Eleven

Why would anyone want to become an opera singer? More surprising still, why would good-looking young graduates, articulate and obviously intelligent, choose such a stony path while their contemporaries hurried down the highway that leads to secure jobs and company cars.

For, in the firmament of singing, every generation breeds its sun, its Callas, with his or her associated circling satellites, less bright no doubt, but stars none the less, and greeted as such by the audiences at the Met and at Salzburg. Then there are the occasional comets, dazzling flashes of talent that blaze across the sky at Geneva, perhaps, or at Glyndebourne, before self-destructing in painful obscurity. Black holes also are to be found, the unfathomable fastnesses of the opera choruses which, once entered, allow of no return. The three Ns, Nerves, (K)nocking and Nodules, claim their share too.

Comparing Maria, Jane and Isabelle, the casual observer would have found both contrasts and common factors. All three, for example, had more than their fair share of good looks, Maria with her grand and sultry glamour, Jane so svelte and supercharged with the electricity of sex, and Isabelle as slim and supple as a child but with a mobile face that mirrored all the appetites of an adult. All three, too, could switch from the most irresponsible gaiety to the most committed professionalism where their music, truly the core of all three lives, was concerned.

But there the resemblance ended. Maria had been endowed with a massive instrument of a voice, with a range of three complete octaves, from the bottom F of Donizetti's *La Favorite* to the top F of Mozart's Queen of the Night, but had the greatest difficulty in remembering the simplest part. Her costumes were always littered with tiny pieces of paper pinned inside the sleeves, sometimes containing whole pages of dialogue and recitative, but one, memorably, marked with the single word *Si* – 'the story of her life', as Rupert had cruelly and repeatedly whispered to anyone with time to listen to him; a gross slander since Maria, although enjoying a healthy appetite for sex, was by no means promiscuous, for a singer.

Jane, by contrast, suffered from a constant, and apparently insatiable, hunger for new partners, believing each new liaison to be the ultimate experience of romantic love. Indeed, the previous year George had even had to hush up a considerable scandal when she had been found in bed with one of their employers' *wives*, an incident which mercifully had remained hidden from the trade at large. It was one thing to be known for providing accessible young women, but quite another for them to be taking liberties in penetrating the employer's own *sanctum sanctorum*.

Without a naturally fine voice, Jane, by persistent hard work and careful exercising while still at the Royal Northern College of Music, had contrived to lift her act to the point where, after the two obligatory years in the Glyndebourne chorus, she had already sung small principal roles for them. Ed had been similarly employed and there they had met and married. A messy, and ultimately violent, affair with one of the staff directors had seen them both ejected from that operatic Garden of Eden, throwing husband and wife, willy-nilly, into the maelstrom of travelling opera, that widest of categories, embracing as it did both the stately perfections of HRH the Prince Arthur's Troupe down to and including the seedy sub-humanities of the now defunct Grand Alhambra Opera Company.

George's outfit, for which they had now worked for over four years, and which gave them both the opportunity to exercise other talents in direction and stage-management, represented the middle ground.

Isabelle, of the three the best qualified with a post-graduate doctorate in philosophy as well as an MA in music from King's College, Cambridge, would have been deeply insulted if anyone had suggested that her work for various small companies had been won as much by her appearance as by her singing. There was no doubt that she could sing: it was a pleasant light soprano voice, of no great volume, for which generations of wise composers had written highly gratifying parts. And when a producer is casting Susanna, or Norina, or Zerlina, or even Adele (which she couldn't quite manage, not being secure in her top D), why would he choose a hippopotamus when slinky little Isabelle looked as if she could (and would) charm the pants (and the cash) off middle-aged bankers with a penchant for energetic young blondes?

Whereas Maria had spoken Italian from birth and German since high school, and Jane had struggled hard to acquire a reasonably plausible European sound, Isabelle, being a gifted mimic, managed to perform in every language as if it were her own, but without understanding a word of what she sang. This gave her performances a slightly tentative, even defenceless, air that made strong men long to protect her while inciting in their wives an equally strong urge to batter her to death.

And her heart? It was still quite untouched, her concentration being on the hydraulics of love-making, a study to which she had been giving her fullest attention for nearly nine years since her then music master had initiated her, aged fifteen, into the baffling but not unrewarding world of male dependency. While it is not necessarily true that music and sex are inextricably entwined, it is beyond dispute that each are the more intense when combined with the other, at least in the early stages.

Yet, with all their beauty, and artistry, and sheer hard slog, these women scarcely earned a living wage between the three of them. True, Maria supplemented her singing fees with minding an antique shop for a friend, and Jane had a regularly irregular job as a sales assistant in one of the big department stores as well as trying to teach the worst of those who auditioned. Isabelle, being an orphan, at least had a private income from money left her by her parents. But any of them could have tripled their wages simply by walking down to the Job Centre, or by joining one of the opera choruses. So to the question: Why sing?, the answer must be given: Because of some invincible inner compulsion, a lust for music and perhaps for performance, which supports an aching body and a downcast heart through the hungry watches of the night.

Chapter Twelve

Their second performance was a corporate evening at a house called Binthorpe Manor, all diamond-paned case-ments and authentic ivy-hung gables, yet paradoxically set in a busy suburb of Slough. It was a complete disas-ter, mitigated for George only by the reassuring knowl-edge that his employers that night, a Slough partnership of solicitors entertaining their staff, were most unlikely to have any contact with his future employers, county families to a man, further down the line.

For a start, every member of the opera company had received an anonymous letter, each tailored to cause the maximum offence or unease to its recipient. Rupert's, for example, alleged that his last partner had developed Aids, Maria's, that her voice had become as comically slack as her belly, and Tim's, that everyone knew that his singing was as skilful as his acting, and just as much in demand. Tim, being older and more secure than the others, just shrugged when showing the letter to George, whereas Maria, tearful and indignant, had rushed from one colleague to another, shrilly demanding the reassur-ance that, coming from the tainted source of a competi-tor, could never have given her the peace of mind she sought so vainly.

'How was your evening with Lord Harrogate?' asked George sourly, when she had finished wailing about her anonymous tormentor. He had driven a silent Ed back to London, all the more sympathetic to the big man's jealous anguish because he was himself tortured by the picture of Isabelle in the arms of that man divested of his white tuxedo, Isabelle squirming beneath him, Isabelle crying out . . . He had nearly driven the van into the back of a police car on the Hendon by-pass.

Maria giggled nervously. 'Very *strange*,' she said. 'Not a nice man, that lord. Not like my Georges. Have you asked Isabelle about her night?' she added maliciously, and walked away, suddenly more cheerful, having shed her burden of gloom on to George.

From the very beginning of this second show, when the basket broke while being carried on, precipitating Bruno on to the floor, every prop seemed determined to malfunction. First his mask fell off, and then the retractable dagger failed to retract, causing poor Ed to shout out a highly audible *'Fuck!'* when its blunted blade was thumped into his ribcage, and then to miss his entrance as Masetto through needing first-aid on the wound.

Tim, distracted perhaps by the mishaps on stage, kept forgetting to turn the pages of the score so that George, already distraught because of Isabelle, found himself playing blind and, as Maria suggested in the interval, 'apparently deaf as well'. Winston and Jane had eyes only for each other, rather unbalancing an already confusing production. Worst of all, Rupert seemed to have lost his voice altogether, mumbling his aria and sometimes just shambling about the stage, pulling faces at the increasingly restless audience, and wiping a steady stream of sweat from his nose and chin.

Only Isabelle, her hair gleaming in the half-light, her figure transcending the ugly and shapeless peasant costume carefully run up by Jane, saved the evening, using her beauty and sheer energy to overcome the shortcomings of her colleagues. Whenever she danced back on to the stage, George could feel a distinct lift in the audience, an almost palpable renewal of their hopes, and when she left, the equally unmistakable return of their corporate despair.

'Here's your cheque.' The company secretary, a dark man with skewed teeth, held out the envelope with a sneer. 'I suppose we have to pay you.'

'Thank you.' George took it gratefully. He had half expected it to be withheld. The sneer he could take, so long as it came with a cheque.

'I don't think we'll be doing anything like this again,' said the man grimly. 'Not after tonight.'

'Well,' George managed a cheery smile, 'you know where we are.'

Another man, large and with heavy features, was passing. He stopped and stared at George. 'Were you in charge tonight?'

'This is Mr Parrish. The senior partner,' put in the toothy man. It sounded like a warning.

George nodded. 'Yes,' he said. 'I'm in charge.'

The man smiled. 'I've seen *Don Giovanni* perhaps sixty times. I've seen it in Salzburg, I've seen it in San Francisco, I've even seen it outdoors at Turnham Green.'

'You must know it well,' said George, encouraged by the smile.

'I do,' said the man, his smile widening. 'And tonight, I can truthfully tell you, was the worst. Not *just* the worst, not the worst by a whisker, but triumphantly the most God-awful unrepeatedly frightful performance I can ever hope to see. I wanted to thank you personally.'

'Oh?'

'Yes. Because however many times I see it in the future, wherever, whenever, at least I shall know that it can't be worse than the one I paid for to entertain my most important clients. Did I hear you say you had Mr Sinclair's address?' This last to the toothy man, who nodded anxiously. 'Good! Keep it by you. Because if we ever employ this man again, in any capacity . . .'

The toothy man shook his head with an air of absolute confidence. 'We won't, Mr Parrish,' he said. 'We won't.'

Chapter Thirteen

'What do you mean you can't *sing*?'

For their third excursion, which was to include performances both at Taunton and then at Bolitho the day after, George had driven down in the hired van with Jane calmly at the wheel on one side, and Ed hunched up against the door on the other. The atmosphere between the two was heavy with silent reproach, and poor George, caught between them and still with his badly bruised shoulder to match Ed's damaged ribs, had a dreary time of it. Nor had he heard a word from Isabelle.

Their first destination, Ashenden Hall, a mile or two outside Taunton, was a bizarre Victorian jumble of bright red and blue bricks, here a tower with pinnacles, there a jutting wing with ranks of tall oriel windows encrusted with carved stone tracery. Its brown-stained corridors held the unmistakable stink of school – unwashed bodies plus stale feet and cabbage water – but for the opera it had been hired (or maybe even given free) to the Somerset Society for the Infirm, whose every move was charted by an angular, commanding beanstalk of a woman styled The Honourable Mrs Alwyne Brewster. And Mrs Brewster, already swathed in a startling dress of pink chiffon, held in place with diamond lizards, had just finished rebuking George for not checking where to park the van, when Ed had appeared in a distant doorway, gesticulating wildly.

'Please excuse me for a minute, Mrs Brewster.'

'Is that man one of yours?'

'Yes.'

'Well, I hope he won't still be dressed like *that* when my guests start arriving. It is black tie, you know.'

'He's more likely to be in a nightshirt,' said George affably. 'He sings the Commendatore.'

Mrs Brewster wanted to smile, but twenty years of absorbing that concentrated and competitive brand of malice which is such an *amusing* feature of county charitable committees had left her just a little short on humour. 'Ha, ha. I see.'

'Will you excuse me?'

'Someone will be moving that *extraordinary* lorry, I trust? It completely wrecks the approach.'

'As soon as possible.' He hurried through the doorway where he had last seen Ed. It led into their changing room, a dingy brown classroom full of scratched little desks with empty holes once intended for ink-pots. These were ranged in a semi-circle before a wide blackboard dominated by a single word: STET, written in chalk letters half a metre high. The rest of the blackboard was entirely blank except where Tim was grimly rubbing out a final equation. Ed was watching him, but turned on hearing George.

'Well?'

'It's Maria. She says she can't sing!'

The prima donna, who had been standing looking out through a dusty window, turned. 'It's the folds in my mucous membrane. They're full of phlegm.' Her voice was scarcely audible, and she was supporting herself by leaning heavily against a radiator. Her great eyes were misty with the tragedy of it all.

'Maria! I don't care *what* they're full of. You have

got to sing. These people have paid us. There's no one else who can sing it.'

She shook her head dolefully. 'It's no good, Giorgio. I've lost the top. I feel like it's hiding from me. Without you to look after her, Maria cannot sing.'

'But what am I going to say to Mrs Brewster?' he groaned. The full horror of the situation was beginning to affect even the usually resourceful George's speech. He would have to hand the money back! And face that hawk-faced old harridan. But even as he wavered, new thoughts were trickling through his brain, bringing fresh hope to his own membranes. 'Although . . .' he mused aloud.

'Although?' Ed was quick on the uptake. They hadn't worked together for nearly five years for nothing.

'Perhaps we weren't quite ready for the critics.'

'What critics?'

'I'm not sure. Mrs B was talking about _The Times_. One of their people have a cottage near here.'

'That's _right_.' Ed was nodding his head sagely. 'I overheard her saying he was coming tonight, but strictly incognito.' He tapped his nose. Maria stared at him.

'So perhaps it's just as well,' said George, ruminating. 'Particularly if Maria had tried to sing and it hadn't quite worked for her.'

The woman in question cleared her throat, and massaged it gingerly. 'It doesn't feel quite so tight,' she said, in an almost normal timbre.

'Now don't push it,' said George. 'It would be far better not to sing than to risk damaging the instrument.'

'Yes, indeed,' chimed in Ed, nodding his head again.

'Oh, you two!' Maria let out a strident cackle.

Mrs Brewster put a startled head round the door. 'Excuse me,' she said. 'But there's an . . . ah . . . um . . . _coloured_ man in the kitchen. He _says_ he's something to do with you . . . ?'

82

George glared at her. 'He is,' he said frostily. 'He's our leading singer.'

'Indeed?' If he had hoped to shame Mrs Brewster, it was a waste of energy. She merely raised her eyebrows and then turned her attention to Maria. 'Do you need anything?'

'No!' said Maria. 'I am having trouble with my th*rrr*oat.'

'Well . . .' said Mrs Brewster. 'My God! Look at that!' They all turned. Through the window they watched a massive Rolls convertible drive slowly up the drive, on to the lawn, through a rose bed and back on to the gravel in front of the porch. Behind it, deep ruts now bore evidence to the weight of the massive machine.

In the front of the car, in the passenger seat, sat someone vaguely familiar, a lean, middle-aged man who was obviously laughing. But what really held the attention of the watchers in the hall was the driver. It was Isabelle, in the scantiest of bikinis, but with a white Panama hat perched rakishly across her gleaming head.

'*Who is that young woman?*' demanded Mrs Brewster. Who is that bastard? thought George with equal ferocity. And, of course, both could answer the other. For as George braced himself to admit to the identity of another of his cast, Mrs Brewster let out a sizzling hiss before forcing her features into something of a smile. 'Why! It's Mr *Hammerson*!'

'Mr Hammerson?'

'Yes. Clay Hammerson. Our new sponsor. He's the London head of one of the big American banks, and has a house the other side of Coombe Constantine, where you're going tomorrow. *Clay!*' This last effusion was addressed to the passenger who had meanwhile led Isabelle by her elbow into the house.

'*Veronica, darling!*' They banged cheeks and kissed the air noisily. '*Mww! Mww!* I'm doubly privileged.

Because I've brought the star with me.' There was an audible intake of breath, from Maria. 'Mademoiselle de Morny hasn't quite mastered driving my car *yet* – ,' he caught George's frosty eye and winked, 'but I'm sure the school governors will allow me to repair any lasting damage.'

'This is Clay Hammerson,' said Isabelle, leading him up to George. 'He was in the audience last week.' Of course! The man in the white tuxedo. 'George Sinclair, our boss.'

'A real live impresario!' The banker managed to make this sound an insult. 'It's a pleasure to meet one.'

'Likewise,' drawled George, shaking his hand and enduring a furious pinch from Isabelle.

'And this is Edmund Nuneham and, er, Maria . . .'

'Cellini,' put in George hastily.

The banker parted his thick lips in something like a smile. 'I imagine you will be needing to rehearse,' he said. 'Let me know if you need anything. We want tonight to be a success.' He took Mrs Brewster's hand as if that were the most natural of gestures, and led her uncomplaining out into the garden.

'Smooth bastard,' muttered Ed.

'He's really very sweet,' said Isabelle.

'When did he pick you up?' said George, trying to sound unconcerned.

'My throat!' growled Maria.

'What about it?' said Isabelle. 'Here, let me look.' And to the others' astonishment, Maria meekly let the younger woman prise open her jaws and peer into the abyss. 'Well!' Isabelle took a step back. 'There's a very simple old-fashioned remedy for *that* . . .'

'Hello, darlings!' It was Rupert, strolling in from yet another door, dressed as if for tennis in white flannel trousers and a cream-coloured games jersey sporting a red and grey school ribbon. 'That's a very snazzy car parked out there in the herbaceous border. Anybody I might know?'

'Wrong faction,' said Ed maliciously. 'That's Isabelle's newest admirer.' He shot a slippery sideways glance at George, who was preserving an impermeable sang-froid.

Rupert shrugged and unleashed his most innocently charming smile. 'You'd be *so* surprised, dear Ed,' he said, 'to know how many sportsmen play for both teams. And sportswomen too.' This last was directed with a tiny toss of his exquisite head in the direction of Jane who came bustling in with a bundle of costumes.

'What the fuck . . .?' Ed, his face screwed up with rage, made to grab him, but George managed to get between them.

'Now, boys!' He also managed to keep his voice cool. 'It's too hot a day for all this. Ed, could you get the rest of the lights? Rupert, you and Maria should run through your recits together. We don't want any more ten minute silences on stage! I'd better help Jane move the truck before Mrs Brewster blows her fuse. Oh, look! There's Bruno's taxi now! I'm sure he'll look after your throat, Maria.' By sheer force of busy necessity, he managed to split them all up and get them occupied by the business of the day, namely presenting *Don Giovanni* to one hundred and forty of the best and most musically refined among Taunton's citizenry.

'Don't they have *hands*? Is this an audience of bloody paraplegics?' Bruno was rubbing his hair vigorously during the interval, while Maria, her face drained of colour, sat staring silently at some brown stains on the classroom wall. Clearly the best and most musically refined citizens of Taunton had somehow evaded the performance, leaving in their place one hundred and forty lobotomized simpletons for whom the simple mechanics of applause would always remain a mystery.

'Here's the tea.' George closed the door with a backwards kick and laid the tray of steaming plastic cups on a desk. Sensing the atmosphere in the room, he added, sympathetically, 'Not very lively, are they?'

'Did someone say they'd paid fifty pounds a ticket?' asked Jane mournfully. Part of Winston's Act One nightshirt had torn in the struggle again and she was patiently restitching it with some beige thread.

'Georges.' Isabelle came up to him and placed both hands on his shoulders. He gazed down into the intense blue of her eyes.

'What?'

'When I'm in the middle of singing "Batti, batti" by Mozart, could you please stick to the score, and not wander off into variations on "Pagliacci"?'

Poor George! He had hoped no one had noticed. 'I'm so sorry,' he said. 'I can't think what happened.'

'It was when she was singing straight at the gent with the big motor car,' put in Ed helpfully. 'I was wondering what you were going to give me.'

'*Otello?*' said Rupert sweetly. Jane and Winston were whispering together in the opposite corner.

Ed glanced across at his wife and then turned back to Rupert. 'I'm not sure when or where,' he hissed, 'but I'm afraid I'm going to have to hurt you. Quite badly. And quite soon.' Having said which, the big man stood up and lumbered out of the room.

'We-ell!' Rupert, his face pale, managed a little show of indifference. 'Temper, temper.'

'Now I think about it,' mused Bruno, who had been watching them all with interest, 'didn't Ed have some sort of bust-up with George's competitor, that chap who ran off, the Alhambra manager?'

'What?' Jane had come across for the sugar. 'Bloody little Steve Boden?'

'Thanks to whom we're here tonight!' put in George.
'He never gave Ed his cheque for the last *Messiah*. Ed said he was going over to discuss it with him. But he never got the chance.'

George raised his cup of tea. 'To absent friends! May all my competitors emulate his excellent example!'

'I'll drink to that!' A neat silver flask had suddenly appeared in Rupert's right hand, and he proceeded to suck at it greedily.

'Rupert!' George grabbed at the flask, which just as suddenly vanished back into the folds of a voluminous waistcoat.

'Don't worry!' Rupert gave him a bright smile. 'Just a dropette to keep Rupie alert.'

'I'm not worrying,' snapped George, for whom this particular battle had ever to be fought at full throttle. 'But I'm not sure whether Tino has his costume ready or not.'

Rupert shrugged, but there was something sagging about his face that impelled Isabelle to go over and hug him briefly. 'Don't worry,' she said. 'The audience love you. You sang the aria so beautifully.'

He beamed. 'It did go rather well.'

'Especially the first verse,' said Maria from the wall.

Rupert's mouth fell. 'The first verse! The *first* verse? What was wrong with the *second* verse, then?'

'It was all fine,' said George quickly. 'Maria is just joking. Look, she's laughing.'

Outside on the plantainous lawns, there was less praise for the great tenor.

'What a weaselly little voice,' said one, a tall, belly-led man in a moth-eaten velvet jacket and no tie.

'Megawimp!' agreed Clay Hammerson, freshly changed (courtesy of the headmaster, who had been charmed by the banker's buccaneering manner) into his white tuxedo. 'I'm surprised they couldn't find someone better.'

'Especially considering what we had to pay them!' said Mrs Brewster, joining them. 'Or rather,' this with a simpering smile quite out of keeping with her jaw, 'what *you* have generously offered to pay them, Clay.'

'It's nothing,' said Hammerson with airy nonchalance. 'The fat Italian tart's good. Do you know?' His eyes were bright with malice. 'After the last performance, she spent the whole night yelling the house down in Bobby Harrogate's bedroom?'

'*No!*' Mrs Brewster was riveted.

'Yes! They say that pianist fellow makes a bit on the side hiring out his sopranos.'

'And *your* friend,' added the tall man enviously. 'What a voice!' And the way he said it suggested something quite else.

Hammerson beamed. If he had not yet managed to bend Isabelle's body to his, he certainly wasn't going to admit that to other elderly voyeurs. There was something about her, a suppleness, an ease of movement, a certain sinuous wiggle in her walk, which had instantly produced in him a hunger for her, a sickness that invaded his belly and kept him uncomfortably aware of his urgent need to invade her bodily. A rich man, he was used to being able to pay for his appetites, especially in women. Of every shape, they were, in his experience, one of the cheapest forms of pleasure, since so many were happy to settle for, preferred even, a kind word and a careful caress rather than the hard cash which might have suited him better. And there was always a right price, if one could only pitch it accurately. Nor did he begrudge them the money or think the less of them for accepting. What counted for him in bed, as in business, was success. If it wasn't exactly love that consumed him, it was something close enough to engender feelings of genuine generosity.

'I believe,' said Mrs Brewster carefully, 'that that man turning the pages is their other tenor.'

'The one who looks like a frog?' asked Hammerson.

'Yes. That's him.'

'That's easy then. I'll tell Sinclair to put him on for Act Two.'

'Can you do that?'

Hammerson smiled. 'Money talks,' he said. And he strode off into the school.

Yet when he found George, he found him strangely resistant to such sovereign suggestion.

'Change Don Ottavio in mid-opera? I don't think we can do that.'

'Nevertheless,' said Hammerson, in a deliberate tone, 'that is what needs to be done.'

George shook his head, partly out of disbelief that his ruse with Tim could have landed him in such a predicament, but partly also at the lean man's invincible self-importance. 'I'm afraid not. I'm sorry to disappoint you.'

'I'm sorry, too,' said Hammerson, growing rather red in the face. 'Let me put it plainer. I'm not asking you. I'm telling you. I'm paying for tonight's performance, and tomorrow's. You will do as I say.'

'Whatever your relationship with my employers,' said George, striving to maintain a tone of reason even though his head was boiling with angry retorts, 'you have nothing to do with the opera company. My contracts are specifically with Mrs Brewster and Mrs Bolitho. But even if you were a party to the contract, which you're not, the casting would still rest with the company. And that's me.' He may have meant to smile, but it came out as an ugly grimace, a baring of the teeth which served only to increase the banker's fury.

'*If* that tenor sings in Act Two . . .' But Isabelle, finding the two men in her life arguing fiercely, weighed in on George's side, albeit for a different reason, namely her loyalty to Rupert. The banker, having a clear perception of his priorities, decided to withdraw as gracefully as he could, though not without promising himself a second bout with George on other, firmer ground.

Chapter Fourteen

After an uncomfortable night in one of the Spartan dormitories of Ashenden Hall, on a sagging mattress supported by a rusty iron bedstead that creaked alarmingly whenever he moved, George set off alone in the van for Bolitho, Ed and Jane having been offered a lift by Clay Hammerson's secretary, Alison Cook, an attractive young woman with a firm chin and clear green eyes, who had been helping Mrs Brewster with the catering and who kept telling them how *surprised* she had been by last night's high standard.

'Did you expect us to be so bad, then?' George had asked her with an unconcealed edge to his voice.

'Oh, no!' she had protested. 'Mr Hammerson had said how *wonderful* it had been at Almondsbury House. But one does hear funny things about some small companies, doesn't one?' And George could hardly disagree.

The countryside had a battered look, not because the threatened storm had broken, but because it had not. The air was sultry, and trees, crops and hedgerows were all wilting in the unaccustomed heat. Even the road seemed to have opened new cracks, and the van lurched along unhappily, with its radiator dangerously close to boiling over. The cabin was stifling, and when he opened the windows, the stinking fumes of the lorries ahead only added to his discomfort. Worst of all, he could feel a cold coming on, the sort of summer cold which clogs the head and makes the heat doubly oppressive.

By noon he was beside the Bolitho gateposts. Too early by at least three hours, he parked behind a small pub beyond the post office, ordered a meat pasty and a refreshing pint of cider, swallowed both as quickly as he could before sauntering off down a path between two houses signed, quite simply, 'To The Sea'.

The village of Bolitho had a strange closed-in air, with its gaunt granite houses roofed over with heavy blue-grey slates, its windows hidden behind massive shutters. If there were gardens, they lurked behind these uncompromising walls, for each house abutted immediately on to the honeycomb of little lanes, none named, which meandered aimlessly, sometimes in a circle, sometimes just to a dead end.

He remembered reading somewhere that this had been a notorious nest of wreckers, a pitiless community whose looted wealth was built on the deliberate destruction of passing ships, lured by false lights on to the Penpoltho Rocks beyond the Head, their hapless passengers and crew hacked to death by the very people who, struggling through the moonlit surf, must have been welcomed as saviours. How many dripping women and children, believing themselves saved by a miracle, had had to face so lonely and savage a death before a special militia, brought down from Bristol (for no one could trust the local magistrates), had caught and hanged the ringleaders?

And how much of the booty had gone to embellish the great house crouching above the cove, whose white verandah, now that he had reached the surf, George could just see glinting between the sloping pines?

'Black Jack' Bolitho, a giant of a man who had hidden his fleshy lips and a scarred cheek beneath a massive black beard of Old Testament proportions, had always been suspected as the ringleader. But the men convicted had gone grim and silent to the gallows, while 'Black Jack' (the fourth but only surviving son of 'Long Tom') had died, an old man in his bed, on the eve of Waterloo. His own son, the Colonel's great-grandfather, alerted by the screams of the old pirate's mistress, had found the deeds to a whole district of Bristol in the strongbox under the bed. Perhaps those silent wreckers had counted on him to look after their families. If so, their hopes were amply rewarded, though not perhaps in the way they would have chosen. He was reputed to have fathered more than fifty bastards on their grateful widows, peopling the villages of Bolitho, Coombe Constantine and Tredinnick with a bevy of black-haired little villains.

Down on the ocean shore, on sands long since washed clean of those ancient rivers of blood, George carefully untied his shoes and, pulling off his socks, left them all together at the foot of a stunted pine. Then rolling up his trouser-legs, he padded gingerly over the rocky shingle and waded into the surf. The water was icy, and a welcome shock to his jaded nerves. Far out, perhaps almost a quarter of a mile into the Atlantic, he could see the razored stickleback points of the Penpoltho Rocks, their jagged teeth shining amid the spray. Here the air was less thick, less tense, but there was still the same feeling of foreboding, of an atmosphere pent-up and ready to burst. The storm, when it came, would be welcome, even as water on water.

To the south reared up three great cliffs, each one hard upon the next, the 'Brothers', looming relics of the Pleistocene age. Out to sea, he could make out half a dozen fishing boats, the furthest one sporting a jaunty red sail. What greater contrast was there than this, he reflected, to the hothouse claustrophobia of the opera dressing room?

A rising chill in his legs woke him from this happy trance. Retracing his steps, and pausing only to watch a great hawk circling in the distance above the cliffs, he dried his feet as best he could with his handkerchief, pulled on socks and shoes, and climbed back up through the village to where he had parked the van. Nothing had changed, except within himself. The elemental force of the sea had cleared his head. Gone were the summer cold and the sense of depression. Foremost, instead, was a determination to make the next performances worthy of the efforts they had all put into the production. Unlocking the cab, he climbed in, started the engine and steered the van up the drive towards Bolitho Court.

By 6 p.m. it was apparent that his hopes of a successful evening were unlikely to be fulfilled. This time it was Bruno who was complaining about his mucous membrane.

'I can't understand it,' he kept saying. 'The voice was fine until this afternoon. What a *bitch*.'

George, watching him, was quietly wondering how you could get a grip on a mucous membrane, with *both* hands, rip it this way and that, roll it up into a viscous little ball, and then stamp it into the pavement.

'George!' It was Rose, her arms full of lilac for the vase on the stairs.

'Mmm?'

'What *are* you thinking about?'

'Nothing. Why?'

'You had such an odd expression on your face.'

'Oh?' He forced an innocent smile. 'Just wool-gathering.'

'Well, come and help me with these flowers. It'll keep your mind off any other worries.'

'Who's that?'

They were standing under a three-quarter-length

portrait of an elderly man, in profile, standing on the cliff edge, gazing out on a stormy sea. 'That's my great-grandfather, General Henry Bolitho. He built the verandah on the other side, and bought most of the flower paintings in the house.'

'He looks sad.'

'He lost three sons at sea.'

'When did he die?'

'Oh.' She had to peer at the little giltwood label at the base of the frame. 'It says 1924. It seems a long time ago, doesn't it?'

'And this?' A military man, or at any rate, one dressed in khaki, with a lot of medals.

'My grandfather. He taught me how to shoot.'

'Rabbits?'

'No, you idiot. Rifles, pistols. In case the Germans come again.'

'A real enthusiast for European union!'

She laughed. 'He's dead too. Look. This is my grandmother painted by Brockhurst. Isn't it lovely?'

He nodded, amused. To him, it looked like the lid of a chocolate box. 'Nice necklace.'

'It's mine now,' she said. 'She left it to me. Would you like to see it?'

'Perhaps tomorrow.' Panic was rising again. 'I'd better just check on the cast.'

'Dad's giving them a glass of champagne in the Drawing Room to cool them down.'

'*What?*'

'Is that bad?' she asked, startled by his expression. 'I thought it'd be a good way to break the ice.'

'Not if Rupert gets near the bottle,' muttered George ominously. 'Which way's the Drawing Room?'

'We can go round through the Saloon, or the other way round by the Dining Room.'

'Which way's quickest?'

'Out this window and across the courtyard,' she said, laughing, and hauled herself over the sill. By the time he was through, she was already clambering through the window opposite from which sounds of convivial laughter could be heard, led by Rupert's high-pitched whinny. It was even hotter outside than in.

'So you knew Chopper?' the Colonel was saying, his rugged face lit up with bonhomie and champagne.

'God, *yes*,' brayed Rupert. 'Old Chopper! Here's how!'

'And what about *Maisie*!' shouted the Colonel happily, refilling Rupert's glass. 'What about *her*, hey?'

'What about her?' Rupert had suddenly tired of the joke, and was preparing to embark on a new and more dangerous course, that of poking public fun at the Colonel.

'*Rupert.*' George's voice cracked across the room. 'Come here, please.'

The tenor bridled. For one thing, he couldn't even see where his employer's voice was coming from. 'Who do you think—'

'*Rupert.* And Tino. Both of you, please.' The willowy tenor and the short, squat actor looked at each other. 'I'm coming,' said Rupert, defeated. 'Do you really want me to try to climb through this window?'

George, still in the courtyard, shook his head. 'Just find your way back to the dressing room. *Now.*' Judging by Rupert's eyes, it would be touch and go. Ed had hurried over to the window too. 'Take him to the toilet. Make him bring up as much as you can. There's still some of that salt left in the hand-props' trunk.' The big man nodded. Rupert's lapses had this much in common with Don Giovanni's conquests: this wasn't the first, and it wouldn't be the last.

'Anything I can do?' Bruno had caught the prevailing mood of panic.

'Yes,' said George, wiping sweat from his forehead. 'Keep the Colonel happy. Find something you can talk to him about.'

By seven the first cars were beginning to roll up the drive, discharging a steady stream of heavy men and robust little women, the former stifling in dinner-jackets, the latter looking cooler in smart little cocktail numbers.

'Deborah!'

'Chudleigh! *Darling!*'

'Keep moving along!' boomed the Colonel. 'Plenty of iced champagne in the Drawing Room.'

'What a party! It must be years since you had a thrash like this, my dear.' The speaker, a bent old man, leaning on a silver walking stick, was shaking his head at the scene.

'Wonderful of you to come, sir.' The Colonel acknowledged few superiors, but for Sir Arthur Treville, Lord Lieutenant of Cornwall, to have driven all the way up from Goonhilly, was a signal compliment. Every county has at least one similar character, complete with brick-red face set off by a crazy halo of wild white hair. Some even have two. But not every county would accept him as their Sovereign's representative.

'To tell the truth, my dear,' the great man leant forward and nearly toppled over, 'I don't go for music in a big way. But when I heard *you* were having an opera, you of all people, I thought . . .' Another cackling crowd of people flocked in through the door, drowning whatever he was saying in his cracked old voice.

'Do you know Lady Pencarrow? Mr and Mrs Hammerson, our very generous sponsors. And Mr Boy Waterhouse, his partner – or something. Of course you know your host, Colonel Billy Bolitho?' And so it went on, the drinks, the chatter, the bored self-confidence of some, the subdued frissons of social panic for others. 'Am I dressed right?' 'Will Karen disgrace me again?' 'Who are those *awful* people over there?' In short, all the pleasures and pains of an English county in full fig, people who have lived in the same spot for six years, and for six hundred, the newest in their polished Bentley, the grandest in a battered Morris, the latter lackin' gs, the former hadding haitches.

Clay Hammerson, rising transatlantically above such mean social trivia, surveyed the scene with a jaundiced eye over a glass of the Colonel's excellent champagne. His wife, Eve, had been drinking, and Waterhouse, his business partner, had been pestering him all day. Even Alison, perfect, squeaky-clean Alison, the ideal secretary, seemed distant, preoccupied, rushing round this crumbling old house, fiddling with last-minute details instead of looking after *him*. Worst of all, he was beginning to doubt whether Isabelle was really going to deliver herself up to him, despite his carefully calculated bid, and if so, there were changes to be made.

The first act went better than George had schooled himself to expect. For one thing, Maria really excelled herself in the duet with Rupert, more than compensating for the tenor's wobbling warbles. For another, George could see that all was not well between Isabelle and the glowering Hammerson. That in itself was enough to inspire his fingers, however damp, to dance nimbly across the keys, wringing from the Bolitho Bechstein an ecstatic celebration of Mozart which earned him a loud 'Bravo' from old Sir Arthur at the end of the Act.

'That's it!' said the despondent Rupert, when they had been safely back in their changing room for nearly a quarter of an hour, and, stripped to their underclothes, were well on with Mrs Tregeare's tray of tea and scones.

'I'm never going to drink another glass of champagne for the rest of my life!'

'Never?' asked Ed with a twinkle, their quarrel apparently forgotten.

'Well, hardly ever.'

'Come on, you two,' chimed in George cheerfully. 'This is supposed to be *Don Giovanni*, not Gilbert and Sullivan.'

'Mr Sinclair?' His name was spoken in a sibilant hiss, a venomous tone that shocked. Turning he found himself face to face with Clay Hammerson. The banker's lips were working ceaselessly, and he was blinking rapidly, one hand held gingerly by the other, and one of his eyes was badly inflamed. What had happened? George looked round for Isabelle, but she must have left the room earlier. 'Yes, Mr Hammerson.'

'You are a total disgrace, you *fucking* little bastard!'

'Hello,' said Rupert, ambling over. 'I thought the performance was next door.'

Hammerson's congested face was looming over George. 'I'm going to make personally sure that this company never does another show. I'm going to make you bankrupt. I'm going to expose you as the huckstering obscene little runtster that you are, I'm going to—'

'Why, look!' exclaimed Rupert. 'You've got dandruff.' He was pointing with apparent interest at Hammerson's collar. 'Look, guys! This funny fellow's got dandruff as well as bad breath.'

Hammerson turned towards Rupert. 'I know something about you, too,' he said. 'It's my job to know about people. That's why I'm a millionaire and you're a failed tenor riddled with notifiable diseases.'

Rupert blinked. 'What do you know about me?' he asked evenly.

'I know you write obscene letters to people,' hissed Hammerson, 'and since my secretary tells me that's a crime in this country, I'm going to see you're prosecuted for it. And that man – ' he was pointing at a startled Winston, ' – that man has real problems, as of tomorrow.'

'Get out! *Get out!*' Maria, her eyes starting out of her head, was running at him. 'We've got a show on. You can't come in here, upsetting poor Rupert like this. This is for artists only.'

Hammerson put out his hand. 'Well, that excludes you for a start, you fat bitch!' he snarled. 'Make the most of this last Act. Because it's the last time you'll sing. If that's what they call the godawful noise you're making.' And, turning on his heel, he walked out, elbowing his way violently past Jane and leaving the door wide open behind him. In the corridor, half a dozen guests were staring in. Ed walked across and closed the door gently in their faces.

'Wow!' said Jane, rubbing her arm, and Ed nodded.

' "Wow",' he said, 'is about right. "Wow" hits it on the nail.' And, suddenly, they smiled at each other.

Despite this interlude, the second act went as smoothly as the first, better even given that Clay Hammerson was no longer glowering from the middle of the front row. George had had to go in search of Isabelle before they could start, eventually finding her coming out of the 'Ladies' lavatory down past the sculleries. The sextet won loud applause, Jane sang a stunning 'Mi tradi', now restored to the opera in place of the ailing Rupert's second aria, and the smoke machine rose to the occasion by letting loose so massive a cloud of vapour that it entirely enveloped half the audience, bringing a smile even to the Colonel's anxious lips.

As soon as the last and loudest curtain call had ended, George hurried down the corridor, following the sign reading LADIES & GENTS. To his surprise, the room he'd used earlier now boasted a bunch of flowers, a perfume spray and a box of violet tissues. He had no sooner started to undo his zip than a little old lady walked in.

'I beg your pardon . . .' he began stiffly.

'You're in the wong place, young man,' she lisped, and grinned, showing a mass of gum but absolutely no teeth at all.

'I thought—'

'You thought wrong.' Really, there was no arguing with her, especially in view of the violet tissues. He flattened himself against the door to get out past her, and there, screwed into the door panel above her head, was the unmistakable message GENTS.

'Look,' he said, pointing.

She turned, saw the notice and let out a little squealing laugh. 'Oh, deaw, oh, deaw!' This time they managed to collide in the doorway.

'After you,' said George, who was becoming desperate. She sidled out and he shut the door. Once again he pulled down his zip, and once again she walked back in.

'Please . . .'

'It's stwuck,' she said. 'I can't get in. And I wearly must.'

'I know what you mean,' grumbled George, gallantly turning back and coming out into the corridor. There was the door he had seen Isabelle coming out of, and it was firmly labelled LADIES. 'Let me.' He tried the handle. The door was half-open but obstructed in some way. He shoved against it, but it hardly moved. He shoved again.

'What's the matter?' It was Winston, his handsome black face apparently free from care for all Hammerson's threats earlier. 'By the way, your zip's undone.'

George shrugged. He was past caring. 'This door's stuck, and this lady wants to get in.' The old crone beamed toothlessly at them.

'Let me.' Winston laid his shoulder against the door. 'Together now. Jesus! What a stink!'

This time the door did begin to give. One more concerted heave, and they stumbled in, in George's case slipping and sprawling over the cause of the blockage.

Out of sight behind the door, the whole floor was sticky with blood. Clay Hammerson half-sat, half-sprawled on the lavatory seat, his face frozen into a ghastly grin. His feet were wedged now behind the door, and both hands clutched the handle of the Commendatore's sword, most of whose shaft was buried deep in his blood-stained chest. There could be no doubt that he was very dead.

Chapter Fifteen

'Let me try to understand this properly.' Detective Chief Inspector Philip Dyle, a tall man, looking trim and alert despite the heat, with thick brown hair that matched his suit, and a steady ironical smile, had taken over the Colonel's Library, not without some diversionary tactics on the part of its proprietor, who would much have preferred the police to use somewhere less personal, the pantry perhaps, or even the Billiards Room. 'You got the blood on your shirt, jacket and trousers when you slipped over on to the body, and your finger-prints are on the sword because you grabbed it to steady yourself?'

Detective Sergeant Tod Skipwith, short, balding with an air of steadfast scepticism, let out an audible sigh.

'Yes,' said George unhappily. 'That's exactly it. This old bid—'

'Lady Pencarrow,' put in Skipwith.

'Whoever. She kept barging into the Gents. Then she said she couldn't quite get through the door into the Ladies. I tried for her, Winston came along, and the rest you know.'

'Remind me about the sword,' said Dyle, writing down a long note.

'On hire from Bapty's. They specialize in props for performances.'

'Only opera?'

'Oh, no. Films, theatres, television. They've got a great stock, tanks, heavy artillery—'

'Then perhaps we can be thankful you only hired a sword,' said Dyle.

George stared at him. 'Can I go now?' he said. 'These clothes are beginning to stink.'

'DC Penjerrick is waiting outside,' said Skipwith. 'He'll accompany you to your bedroom, and take all your clothes away for testing. He'll give you a receipt of course.'

'Of course.' George couldn't decide which of the two he disliked more, the Chief Inspector with his alarming jokes, or the Sergeant with his accusatory menace.

'The question here, Tod,' said Dyle, tipping back in the Colonel's chair and lighting another cigarette after George had left, 'is not about opportunity. Almost anyone could have slipped out of sight for a couple of minutes.'

'Even the cast?' Skipwith stifled a yawn. It was long past midnight and, Mrs Skipwith having left him some months before for a fellow officer, he had eaten very little since the night before.

'Why not? Don't forget the murder almost certainly took place during the interval. Hammerson was in the front row for the first act, his chair was empty for the second. We'll know about that soon enough. From what I know of singers, they'll all have slipped off to the toilet at some point. What we need here is motive.'

'Money?'

'We'll have to wait till Monday to find out anything about a Will, but his wife,' Dyle consulted some notes, 'Mrs Eve Hammerson, must have had a strong motive.'

'Especially if it's true he was sniffing after that French bint,' said Skipwith with an appreciative grin.

Their first two hours in the building had not been wasted. The murderer could easily have slipped out of the lavatory leaving Hammerson propped up on the seat. It was only once his legs had caused the blockage that had stymied Lady Pencarrow that he was discovered.

'Quite. So ... Colonel Bolitho?'

'He obviously didn't like him, but it's not likely.'

'No, nor the wife or daughter. Nor the housekeeper.'

'I didn't like the look of the business partner.'

'Waterhouse? Nor did I. Fremantle's running checks on him now. The secretary?'

It was the Sergeant's turn to check his notes. 'Alison Cook. Definitely a suspect. All those tears could have been an over-reaction. I'd say he was a bastard to work for. Rest of the audience?'

'The local landed gentry mostly,' said Dyle dismissively.

'That doesn't rule them out!'

'Of course not. They'll all be being put through the computer now, so we can let them go home. But it needs more than just being a newcomer to stir up the neighbours to the point of deliberate murder. He only bought Tredinnick Hall three months ago. A bit soon for a blood feud. Don't forget our man, or woman, was sufficiently alert to wear gloves. The only prints were Sinclair's, and he has two witnesses to back his story about breaking down the door. Unless that was an elaborate ruse, in which case he's our man, this was premeditated. Miss Bolitho and the housekeeper deny having any gloves at all. Mrs Bolitho had two pre-war pairs in a drawer upstairs. They're both there, untouched, though I want them checked anyway.'

'Right. So that leaves the troupe.'

'Precisely.'

'Would they have gloves?'

'That's what I want you to find out. Also, who's

sleeping with who? Who hates who? And why?'

'You think it's like that?'

'It's always like that. Nine or ten adults banged up together, travelling around, working under maximum pressure with minimum comforts. Bunch of psychos by now, as likely as not.' The Chief Inspector had a jaundiced view of entertainers.

Nor was he alone in this. The other side of the courtyard, Mrs Tregeare was holding forth to a fascinated audience of two constables and the scene-of-crime supervisor who had joined her for a cup of good strong tea.

'I heard him,' she said. 'Even though he didn't know it. "You'll regret this," he said. "You lay a hand on her and I'll break your back." Right out loud, just like he was talking to you or me.'

'You ready to swear to that?' Detective Constable Fremantle was sleepily making notes.

'I certainly am,' said the old woman stoutly. 'It was no way to talk to a gentleman like Mr Hammerson. I never liked that Sinclair. He had his eye on Miss Rose, too, you know. Sex mad he is, I'd say!' She couldn't quite remember if they still hanged murderers, but she certainly had her hopes.

Gradually, the guests, having given their details to the small team assembled from Launceston, were drifting reluctantly away.

'I'm so sorry, dear.' Mrs Tensing of Tensing Hall was looming over Mary Bolitho, with a patronizing gleam in her eye. 'Such a disaster for you, and after you'd tried so hard.'

'Nonsense,' growled Sir Arthur, freeing his silver stick from an inconvenient grating, a relic perhaps of some long-defunct and fruitless attempt to heat the tall stone entrance hall in winter. 'Terrific show! These opera chaps are ... *wonderful!*'

106

'I tell you what, Billy.' The Colonel had been button-holed by his neighbour, Major Tensing. 'This place'll be famous. You see. *News of the World*, that sort of thing.'

The Colonel bared his teeth. 'Good to see you, Tensing,' was all he could manage and, turning his back on his departing neighbours, he sought refuge in his Library, only to find it crammed with a lot of strange men who stared at him until he left.

'I'll say this,' he confided in his daughter, without noticing how pale she had become, 'I don't believe Sandy East Finchampstead would have worn a brown tweed suit in weather like this.'

She stared at him. 'What are you talking about, Dad?'

'Sandy East Wotsit. You know. The copper in that book I was reading.'

'Dad!' She was almost shouting. 'You don't understand. It's serious. They think George did it.' And ran upstairs before he could reply.

Chapter Sixteen

Once the police had gone, around 3 a.m., Clay Hammerson's body having preceded them on its way to the postmortem, the household began to drift off to bed. Everyone staying had been told to remain on the premises, and George, when he went to draw the heavy brocade curtains across his bedroom window, saw a solitary constable standing under the tree by the corner of the stables, his face momentarily lit by the flame of a match.

Surely the storm must break soon. The heat was unbearable now. What would it be like once the sun rose the next morning? And how could he sleep at a time like this? With a groan, he flung himself onto the huge oak bed. It was unexpectedly soft, and the linen sheets were cool on his aching legs. He closed his eyes.

When he woke, it was after ten, and even hotter, yet he felt refreshed and bright. Seven hours' sleep! There was a tap on the door. Pulling on his dressing-gown, he padded across the boards and opened it, to find Isabelle, wrapped in a scanty red silk kimono and carrying two mugs of steaming black coffee.

'Hello.'

He smiled down at her anxious face. 'Hello.'

'Can I come in?'

'When have I ever barred you from my room?'

She pushed out her lips into a most entrancing pout,

and handed him one of the cups. 'We must talk,' she said, and herded him back into the room, closing the door behind her. 'Oh! You have a much bigger room than ours.'

'How was your night with Maria?'

She laughed. 'Imagine. Your little sister in bed with your ex-mistress. What *would* dear Papa have said?'

He winced. 'Isabelle. Please.'

'Georges. Please. I love you. You love me. We both know it, and all this drama is good.'

'How so?'

'*How so?* Poor Papa would think you very pompous. Because, *chéri*, it will show what a little thing our misdemeanours are, *toi et moi*, compared to great things like murder. By the way, Georges, was it you who killed that horrible man?'

He laughed. 'Of course not. I was afraid it might have been you.'

'Me?' She opened her dazzling eyes very, very wide. 'Why me?'

'Because I saw you coming out of the murder room just before the second act.'

'That was the murder room?'

'Yes.'

'I thought he was murdered in the ladies loo.'

'He was.'

'But, *chéri*, I was in the men's. The ladies' was *occupé*.'

'No, you weren't,' he said. 'I was there. You came out of the first door on the right.'

'Yes,' she agreed. 'The men's lavatory was first, because I went past it to try the ladies'. There was a big fat woman in there, smelling of gin. She winked at me, so I came out, and went in next door.'

'Oh?' He was trying to remember the geography. 'Didn't it have a sign on it?'

'Yes,' she said patiently. 'It read ... oh ... "Gentleman's"?'

'Or "Gents'?"'

'Precisely.'

George sat down and looked up at her in silent thought. 'So,' he said at last. 'Either you killed him, or someone changed the signs.'

'Why would anyone change the signs?'

'I don't know. What made him so angry in the interval?'

She blushed, a beautiful sight. 'Oh, Georges. It is hard to tell a brother these things.'

'Try.'

'He caught me going back to the changing room and said he had to talk to me.'

'And?'

'He took me down that other corridor and into a room with a big green table—'

'I'm not interested in the furniture,' snapped George. 'Tell me what happened.'

'But, you see ... Well, he pushed my face down on to the table, and then pulled up my skirt from behind.' She hid her face.

'And?'

'Luckily it had a soft top.'

He stared. 'What did?'

'The table. I told you. It was green, and furry.'

'Isabelle. *Please*. What happened? Did he ...?'

'Did he what?'

'Did he penetrate you?'

'Oh, you *English*! You have such funny words.'

'Isabelle, I swear, if you don't tell me now, I'll murder you too.'

She giggled at him between her fingers. '*Georges!* Is it likely I'd let a ridiculous man like Monsieur Hammerson have what I keep for my *chéri*? I back-kicked him

110

between the legs and then poked him in the eye on my way out. *Quel crapaud affreux!*' She let out a peal of laughter. 'Now are you going to murder me too?'

'I hope not,' said the Chief Inspector putting his head round the door. 'Because I need both of your statements. I'll start with Miss Morny if you can spare her for an hour or two more?' He fixed George with his sardonic smile. 'Then perhaps you could come down to the Library when you're dressed, Mr Sinclair?'

'Of course,' said George. 'You appreciate that what she said was a joke?'

The Chief Inspector smiled. 'Oh, yes, sir,' he said. 'We all appreciate a joke round here.'

When George was called into the Library an hour later, he found it buzzing with activity. Passing the Dining Room next door, he could see that that had also been taken over, as the Scene-of-Crime office, with half a dozen computers set up under the steady gaze of an elderly woman in jeans and a fishing sweater who stared at him as he passed.

In the Library, Dyle was set up behind the big desk on which sat a tape-recorder operated by a young police-woman in uniform, while Skipwith was in his favourite position, lounging against the windowsill.

'Come in,' said Dyle. 'I think we'd better make this formal, don't you?'

'Is it really up to me?' asked George, momentarily nonplussed.

Skipwith leant forward. 'It's for your own protec-tion,' he said. 'And believe me, you need it. Please sit down there.'

The policewoman switched the recorder on, position-ing the microphone midway between Dyle and the chair which had been indicated.

'This interview commencing eleven oh eight hours, Sunday, May the eighteenth, DCI Dyle interviewing, DS Skipwith and WPC Wells in attendance. Your full name and date of birth, sir?'

George stared at him. Was this really happening? 'George Tassilo Sinclair. May the eighteenth, nineteen sixty-two.'

'Happy birthday,' said Skipwith, and sniggered into his handkerchief.

'May I have the spelling on the middle name?'

'T-A-S-S-I-L-O.'

'Family name?'

'I presume so.'

'Now, Mr Sinclair, I'm going to read to you from this card, and I want you to tell me if you understand. Right?'

George nodded. Dyle stared at him. 'Right,' he added hastily. 'Right.'

Dyle put on his reading glasses, and scanned a thick square of card. 'You do not have to say anything. But if you do, and mention now something which you later use, or cause to be used, in or for your defence, the Court may, if it so chooses, decide that your failure to mention it now strengthens the case against you. A record will be made of anything you say and it may, or may not, be given if you are brought to trial.' He looked up over his glasses at George, who preserved a complete silence. 'Do you understand?'

'No,' said George, truthfully.

'I'll read it again,' said Dyle. 'Please listen carefully. You do not have to say anything. But if you do, and mention now something which you later use, or cause to be used, in or for your defence, the Court may, if it so chooses, decide that your failure to mention it now strengthens the case against you. A record will be made of anything you say and it may, or may not, be given if you are brought to trial.' He looked up over his glasses at George, who was frowning at him. 'Now do you understand?'

'No,' said George, 'but I'll say I do if it helps us get on.'

'He's read you the caution,' snapped Skipwith. 'It's perfectly clear. What's the problem?'

'It's the bit about mentioning. I don't see how if I do mention something, I can be said to have failed to have mentioned it.'

Dyle stared at the piece of pasteboard. 'Blast!' he said. 'Ruby's typed it out wrong again. Thank you, Mr Sinclair. You're absolutely right. It should read: "But if you do, and do NOT mention now something which you later use, or cause to be used, in or for your defence," et cetera, et cetera . . .'

'That's all right then,' said George, relieved. 'I understand it now.' Skipwith let out a strange sort of droning sound beside the window. He was staring at George all the time.

'Let's get the background straight first,' said Dyle. 'You own this travelling opera outfit?'

'I'm not sure "own" is the right word. I hire the other singers, pay the running expenses and sell the performances. Any difference is my profit.'

'Or loss?'

George smiled. 'I wouldn't do it if I was going to make a loss.'

Skipwith leant forward. 'No businessman wants to make a loss, any more than any criminal wants to get caught. But it happens.'

George stared back. 'Meaning?'

'Hammerson threatened to put you out of business, didn't he?' said Dyle.

'We've got four statements here,' added Skipwith, crossing to the desk and brandishing some papers. 'That's what they all say.'

George shrugged. 'That's not a secret,' he said. 'He was in a dreadful state last night. He was threatening everyone.'

'Not everyone has their fingerprints on the murder weapon,' said Dyle, with a disconcerting chuckle.

'A Mrs Brewster telephoned to say you had quite a row with him Friday night,' mused Skipwith.

'He was trying to interfere with the casting.'

'That's your prerogative?'

'Of course.'

'Tell me where you found Mr ... Wheeler.'

'He came to an audition we held in Fulham.'

' "We"?'

'I also employ Mr and Mrs Nuneham backstage. They help me choose new singers.'

'Are they the only members of your cast who've been with you before? Apart from Miss Cellini?'

'Yes.'

'Why's that?'

George smiled wryly. 'The four others I had last year have formed their own company. They're doing a musical revue based on favourite arias.'

'What do they call themselves?'

'Opera Strip, if you must know.'

'Getting much work?' Skipwith sounded genuinely interested.

'Mostly abroad,' said George. 'We don't keep in touch.'

'Getting back to Mr Wheeler,' said Dyle casually. 'What else do you know about him?'

'Not much. He was born in Huddersfield. He's got a fine voice.'

'I'm told he's humping Mrs Nuneham.'

'You'll have to ask her,' said George, flushing.

'I don't need to,' said Skipwith. 'They were doing it in front of an open window last night. My constable said it was better than the late-night movie.'

114

'And Miss Morny,' carried on Dyle, in the same even tone, 'tells me that you and she are lovers, although Miss Cellini told me the same thing.'

George shook his head. 'That's both right and wrong,' he said. 'I understand you have to get the background, but these are our private affairs. And they are misleading. In this business, on the road, people do tend to get involved. But only infrequently. It's usually very light-hearted. I think you've got the wrong idea.'

'Mr Hammerson certainly did. Miss Morny told us what happened in the Billiards Room.'

'He was a very unpleasant man.'

'Why did you tell him you'd break his back?'

George's mouth dropped open. 'Why did I say *what*?'

'Why did you say, and I quote: "You'll regret this. You lay a hand on her and I'll break your back"?' When he had finished reading, Dyle raised his eyes to meet George's. 'Take your time,' he said kindly. 'If it helps, I don't think Mr Hammerson was my cup of tea either.'

George shook his head. 'It doesn't help,' he said, 'because I never said that to him.'

'We have an independent witness,' said Skipwith triumphantly, 'whose sworn statement is here,' he brandished a sheet of paper, 'who positively identifies you as having said that to him.'

'Me?' George's face was screwed up in concentration. 'Mind you,' he said, in a burst of candour, 'I'm not saying I wouldn't have liked to say that to him, after Isabelle told me about his attack on her this morning . . .'

'When you said that you would murder her *too*?'

'As a joke.'

'Yes, I'd forgotten it was a *joke*. But those were your words, weren't they?'

'You were there. You heard how I said it.'

'Joking apart, Mr Sinclair,' and Dyle's voice held a

115

sharper edge now, 'there aren't too many different ways of saying you're going to murder somebody *too*.'

'Yes, there are,' protested George, suddenly nervous. 'You could say it meaning that would be a second person to be murdered . . .'

'And?'

'Yes,' conceded George, 'you could say it meaning the second person you yourself had murdered.'

'And which,' asked Skipwith, 'did you mean, *sir*?' He hadn't taken his eyes off George throughout the whole interview. He must have been sick of the sight of him.

George sighed. 'The first,' he said, and suddenly his eyes lit up. '*Of course! I've got it.*'

'Sir?' Dyle was watching him narrowly.

'Those words. The ones I was supposed to have said to Hammerson.'

'What about them?'

'Go back and ask your witness if he actually saw the two of us together. I have a rather silly habit – I'm quite ashamed to admit it – but I do tend to talk to myself quite a bit. Mostly imaginary rows, arguments, you know the sort of thing . . .'

'No,' said Skipwith sourly. 'We don't.'

'You must,' said George. 'Lots of people talk to themselves. I do it so often it doesn't register. If it was me they heard, then I'll bet I was alone, and I was just day-dreaming. He'd been sniffing after Isabelle for some time. It was very distasteful.'

Dyle and Skipwith looked at each other. He'd mentioned this idea on the very same tape as the caution. It was both plausible, and very irritating. It had been their best shot, and suddenly it seemed rather feeble.

'I think that's all for now, sir,' said Dyle, rewarding George with a warm smile. 'You've been most helpful. We'll talk again later. In the meantime, we'd like to see Mr Wheeler if you can find him for us.'

When George had left the Library, his heart still thumping, he walked down the corridor only to meet the Colonel, his face redder and angrier than ever, marching in the opposite direction, discussing something with Hammerson's secretary, who was carrying a bowl of used raffle tickets.

'This house is becoming unbearable,' the Colonel, seeing George, snapped at him. 'I wish you could keep your troupe in order.' And even from where they were standing, the sound of people shouting at each other in the Tapestry Room could be heard.

Hurrying in, George found Maria and Rupert locked in some furious embrace, while the others looked on, exhausted, but obviously part of the altercation. Tim, for once, was actually smiling. George grabbed Maria, who was tugging at the tenor's hair, and pulled her away from him. 'Stop it,' he shouted. '*Stop it!*' An uneasy silence fell. 'What is the matter?'

'I didn't write those poisonous letters,' squeaked Rupert, who was anxiously massaging his throat. 'I've told them that I didn't.' He looked as if he was about to burst into tears. 'I don't know why he said that—'

'You liar!' spat Maria. 'You write those ugly things. *Pédé!*'

'He must have had some reason,' mused Ed, his eyes on Rupert's face. 'Surely he wouldn't have made up something so improbable . . .'

'You mean like calling Maria a fat bitch who can't sing?' said Rupert with something of a revival of his usual form. Jane laughed, precipitating a further string of insults from the enraged Maria. 'All right,' said Rupert reasonably. 'I *do* know what he meant. I did write some rude letters about someone he perhaps knows, knew rather, a City banker who messed me about, and I mean *messed me about*. I got a list of partners in his firm and I also sent them some naughty photos of him and me.

It gave me a lot of satisfaction. There! Satisfied? I've got better things to do than stick a lot of newspaper clippings together to tell you all things you know already. Everybody knows everything in this company.'

'Well, I for one don't know what he meant about Winston,' put in Ed helpfully. 'What was all that about?'

Winston continued to stare at the floor. 'Who knows?' he said, after a very long silence. 'Meant nothing to me.'

'Oh, that reminds me,' said George. 'Chief Inspector Dyle wants to see you, Winston. In the Library, right out of here and last door on the left.'

'I think,' said Jane, when Winston had left, 'that George, being the boss, had better sort out what happens next. I, for one, can't sit here indefinitely while the plods try to find the hero who killed that awful man. I also want to know what happens to our next show, which, in case you've all forgotten, is next Friday.'

'And while you're about it,' said Bruno, turning to George, 'I'd like my wages up to and including last night's show.'

'But—'

'And I'm speaking for everyone. We'd all like to be paid. A cheque will do. Tomorrow morning will do. That's the bottom line.'

'But—'

'Come on, George.' This was Jane joining in again. 'We all know you've been paid. Normally no one would worry, you're a good payer. But with this murder . . . You must see.'

George looked round at them. He did see. 'Right,' he said. 'Give me two hours. I'll get it done now.' No one had anything else to add.

*

Poor George! How could he think about money when half the household suspected him of skewering his most recent sponsor to death in the downstairs ladies' lavatory?

But think about it he did, settling down at the desk in his bedroom and drawing up two columns with the help of his cheque book and a small black diary. The first (and shorter) was entitled 'Income' and the second (and longer) 'Expenses'.

Altogether he had received ten nine-hundred-pound deposits amounting to nine thousand pounds, and now the balance of the first five performances adding just over another twelve thousand: a grand total of twenty-one thousand four hundred pounds paid in, with just over two thousand still to come for last night. So far, so good. The second column read:

Hire of church hall (6 days)	600
Deposit on Venice holiday	899
Advance to Bruno	100
Repairs to Citroën	1,540
Mr Sumption (*répétiteur*)	135
Jane's producer fee	500
Hire of costumes	1,495
Hire of van	535
Artur Louis	1,950
Props	472
Petty cash	213
Stamps and stationery	78
Back rent on flat	3,000
Other	9,347
	20,864

Add to that the singers' fees, over seventeen thousand pounds in all, plus petrol and miscellaneous running costs, against only another ten thousand pounds to come in from the remaining four performances, even assuming

119

the police would release them to fulfil their contracts, and the picture was not good: £33,500 in, £38,000 out. And nothing more to come – at all.

Last month's euphoria (when he had gone off and bought Isabelle that absurdly extravagant dress from Artur Louis) was being replaced by this month's terminal depression. And the problem could clearly be laid along the line marked 'Other'.

'Other' indeed! What did it contain that was not in some way connected with getting closely acquainted with his sister? Flowers from Pulbrook, dinners chez Nico, a weekend at Hambleden, more flowers, more dinners and that saucy little necklace, whose violet amethysts had winked so charmingly the night he fastened the diamond clasp around her slender thigh in the undergrowth on Clapham Common. In fact, he had squandered a normal year's income in three short weeks during which his prime, indeed almost sole, occupation had been the energetic and repeated commission of an imprisonable crime!

Even at this moment, he had managed to run up an overdraft of over three thousand pounds, against about fourteen hundred left in his deposit account, and all secured on those flimsy contracts. How could he play for them if he wasn't allowed to leave Bolitho? How, for that matter, could he play for them if he was in *prison*?

There was a tap at the door. He pretended not to have heard, saw the handle turning, and then heard another, more peremptory, knocking.

'Who is it?'

'It's me. Rose.'

Sighing, he rose and walked across, unlocking the door and trying to assume a welcoming smile. 'Aren't you afraid to enter the room of the chief suspect?'

She walked past him with a cheerful grin. 'I can't imagine you killing anyone,' she said briskly. 'Not even Mr Hammerson.' Hearing footsteps, he quickly closed the door again. The footsteps went past.

120

'I'd like to have punched him on that silly nose.'

'That's honest of you,' she said. 'So should I. But I think we'd better keep those inclinations to ourselves, don't you? There wouldn't be that much fun in beating up a corpse.' They glanced at each other and started to laugh at the preposterous thought of Hammerson at their mercy in a shroud. 'What's all this?' Before he could stop her, she had leant over the table and picked up his balance sheet. 'Oh dear!'

'Just some figures.' He took the paper from her and laid it back face down on the table.

'Please forgive me. I shouldn't have looked. My mother always says I'm incurably nosy.'

'It's not interesting.'

'It is to me.' She met his stare with a frankness that momentarily shocked them both into silence.

'I . . .' But she was already in his arms, straining up to kiss his lips. Now someone else was banging on his door. Quickly disengaging herself, she laid a finger on his mouth before disappearing inside the massive wardrobe between the windows and pulling its door shut behind her.

'Who is it?'

'It's me. Open the door.' Maria!

With an exasperated sigh, George crossed the room and unlocked the door, but any thoughts he might have had of blocking her entry were frustrated by her imperiously sweeping past him.

'So! You have a bigger room than I!'

'But you've got a better view of the sea.' George always kept a careful note of morale-boosters where his singers were concerned, the war against their complaints being a ceaseless one.

'I have a friend who's a lawyer.' Her great eyes were fixed upon him with tragic strength.

'And?'

'Oh, Giorgio! You are such an idiot. I know you.

You killed that banker because he insulted your Maria. No, don't speak. Maria knows. But there was no need. I was amused by all his nonsense. But now it is for me to defend you.'

'Maria.'

'*Si, carissimo?*' She had sat down on the bed, and now opened her capacious arms to him. 'Come, let Maria comfort you . . .'

He stayed firmly in front of the cupboard. 'Please understand that I did not kill Mr Hammerson.'

'Maria understands.' There was a maddening complacency about her acceptance of his guilt.

'No,' he almost shouted. 'Maria does *not* understand. I did *not* kill him, though I certainly felt like—'

There was more creaking in the corridor, followed by a timid tapping on the door. Maria put her finger to her lips before slithering under the bed with an unexpected ease. Surely there would hardly be room? The tapping was repeated. 'Who is it?'

'Shh! It's me, Isabelle.' How many more? With an air of hopeless resignation, he opened the door and fastened it behind her. 'I must see you.'

'Come in. I think there's a space left behind the curtains.'

'What?'

'Nothing.' He was wiping his forehead. 'Why are you here?'

'Because I had to see you.'

'Well, here I am.' He evaded her embrace and returned to his position in front of the cupboard, which had suddenly creaked.

'What's that?'

'What?'

'That noise.'

'What did you want to say to me?'

122

'Oh, Georges. To use such a tone with me.' The bed let out a melancholy twang.

'There's someone there! I know there is.'

He was spared the need to answer by an unmistakably official hammering on the door. 'Mr Sinclair. *Mr Sinclair!*'

'Come in. Come in.' He flung the door open. If they'd come to arrest him, it could only be seen as a merciful release.

There were four of them, led by the solid figure of Detective Chief Inspector Dyle. 'I haven't got a warrant, Mr Sinclair. But I should like to search your room.'

George shrugged. How many times must such a search have proved a tedious chore? But this time . . . 'Please, feel free,' he said. And it said something for his commitment to providing live entertainment that, with the prospect of such personal embarrassment ahead of him, part of him could still be amused at what the officers would find.

Chapter Seventeen

'*Three* women, Mr Sinclair?' As usual the Chief Inspector was smiling. They were safe now, away from the shouting, back in Colonel Bolitho's Library. George sat in the same chair across the desk from him, with the same tape-recorder between them, while Tod Skipwith lounged this time against a tall bookcase stuffed with old maps and inventories, but staring, as was his custom.

'I'm sure you realize it was not what it seemed.'

'Let me see. The French girl was in your arms, yelling that she would protect you ...?'

'Well—'

'And Miss Rose Bolitho was in your cupboard insisting she would protect you ...?'

'Er—'

'And then we found the large Italian lady stuck fast under your bed, and from what we could understand from her caterwauling—'

'Which wasn't much—' put in Skipwith.

' ... she wanted to protect you too.'

'But I don't need protecting from anything,' said George angrily. 'I didn't *do* anything.'

'I think,' said Dyle, with a dry smile, 'you may now need a bit of protection even so ... from the three ladies!' Both policemen laughed heartily, while George stared stonily at the desk. Was this sort of thing really allowed? 'Seriously, though,' Dyle pushed a button on the recorder, 'this second interview with George Tassilo Sinclair commenced sixteen eighteen hours Sunday, May eighteenth, DCI Dyle interviewing, with DS Skipwith in attendance, covered by the same caution recorded on tape number three oh seven, stroke one. Now, tell us about your movements yesterday evening.'

'It was very simple,' said George wearily.

Dyle leant forward slowly, showing no sign of his sudden inner excitement. It was amazing how often the killer succumbed to an urge to tell everyone how clever he, or more rarely she, had really been. 'Tell me about it,' he said, with unfeigned interest.

'I arrived with the van at about three o'clock. We'd been staying the night near Taunton in hostility—'

'I'm sorry?' Dyle was staring at him.

George laughed. 'Hostility. It's what we in the trade call the dreaded "hospitality" some people offer instead of hotel accommodation. Camp beds in the attic, nylon sheets and make your own breakfast, that sort of thing.'

'Very comical,' murmured Skipwith.

'I got here early and had lunch at the pub in the village—'

'The Bolitho Arms?' put in Dyle.

'I dare say. Pasty and chips, and a pint of Old Whimsical. I walked down through the village to the cove and sat by the sea for half an hour. Then, as I say, I collected the van—'

'Who was here when you arrived?'

'Rose Bolitho was waiting in the hall. She showed me to my bedroom, and then helped me carry some of the costumes to the green room.'

'That, for the official record, is the Tapestry Anteroom marked three on this plan. I'm showing you.' Dyle pushed a neat and very detailed sketch of the floor-plan of Bolitho Court across the desk, and George stared at it.

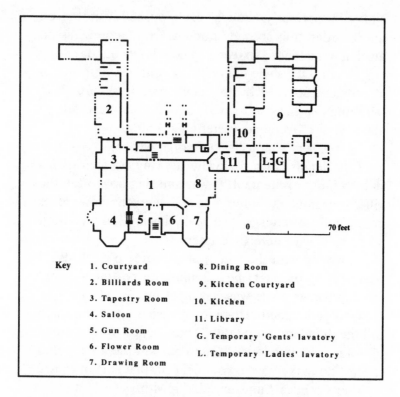

Key

1. Courtyard
2. Billiards Room
3. Tapestry Room
4. Saloon
5. Gun Room
6. Flower Room
7. Drawing Room

8. Dining Room
9. Kitchen Courtyard
10. Kitchen
11. Library
G. Temporary 'Gents' lavatory
L. Temporary 'Ladies' lavatory

At last he looked up. 'Yes,' he said. 'That's correct. I'm not very good at maps, I'm afraid.'

'Just tell us the facts,' said Dyle, bored. It was clear now he wasn't getting a confession, not yet anyway.

'Your bedroom is the one marked number seven above the Drawing Room?'

George looked carefully, then nodded. 'Yes,' he said. 'I think that's right. I've got one of those big windows looking towards the sea.'

'Then what?'

George paused to collect his thoughts. 'Bruno was the first to arrive,' he said. 'He'd come by taxi from the Bude bus station. I remember him because the first thing he said to Mrs Bolitho when she went to shake his hand was, "I should tell you I'm allergic to suet." I didn't see the others arrive. We got set up. Rose and Mrs Bolitho showed them to their bedrooms. Mrs Hammerson walked in at one moment. I think she must live in the village?'

'Next village,' grunted Dyle. 'There's a coastal path. How did you know it was Mrs Hammerson?'

'She introduced herself. She was looking for her husband. I think she had some idea he might have driven Isabelle down.'

'And had he?'

George shrugged. 'Who knows? She doesn't tell me her plans.'

Skipwith leant forward. 'I thought she was your girl?'

George's heart thumped hard. 'My girl?'

'She was in your bedroom, wasn't she?'

'Among others.' George was fighting to keep his expression light and guileless.

'Have you slept with her?' This from Skipwith, his lips curled back in a snarl.

George stared at him. 'What's that to you?'

Dyle coughed apologetically. 'It's the sort of thing we do need to know,' he said.

'Then you'd better ask her,' said George defiantly.

'A *gentleman*!' sneered Skipwith, receiving a warning look from Dyle. These things could be overdone.

'Tell us about the interval,' said Dyle. 'There was quite a bit of applause?'

'At the end of Act One? Yes,' acknowledged George, inclining his head, 'yes, there was.'

'A success by your standards?' Skipwith wasn't letting up. This man was apparently involved with three beautiful women while he had to make do with his chilling memories of the absconding Mrs Skipwith. It would be a genuine pleasure to lock him up.

'A success by anyone's standards,' retorted George. 'I took a bow,' he glanced slyly at the red-faced Sergeant, 'but they were calling for more. So I went back in for another bow, and then I went out into the changing room, I mean the Tapestry Room.' He jabbed at the room numbered three with his finger.

Dyle leant forward. 'Who was in the room?'

George screwed up his eyes. 'Rupert was sitting in the corner. His voice was giving him trouble – I think he'd thrown up – and Maria was massaging his throat. Um . . . Ed was listening to the test match on his radio, yes, and Winston was filling in some newspaper questionnaire . . .'

All the time, Dyle was checking this description with his notes from the other interviews. 'Mr Bruno Retz?' he asked, looking up.

George laughed. 'Bruno always goes out in the interval for a quiet cigarette.'

'An opera singer?' Dyle raised his eyebrows.

'Can be good for the nerves. In the short term, that's more important than anything else.'

'Mrs Nuneham?'

'I passed Jane in the doorway. She was going back to collect some discarded costumes once the audience had filed out through the other door.'

'Into room five?'

'Yes. The Flower Room. They passed that way to where drinks were being served in the Drawing Room.'

Dyle put down his pen. 'You seem to know the geography pretty well for a man who only arrived yesterday?'

George nodded. 'That's my job. We use the Flower Room entrance in both Acts.'

'Going round by the Dining Room?' Skipwith was suddenly craning over Dyle's shoulder, staring at the floor plan.

'No,' said George. 'We shin up the main stairs and then abseil down from the roof.'

Skipwith smiled at him. 'I like a smart-ass,' he said. 'Because I like a man who can still laugh when he accidentally breaks his jaw on a paving stone.'

'Can we keep to the essentials?' Dyle suddenly sounded tired. Looking at his face, with its flaccid skin and deeply scored furrows running down on either side of the long beaky nose, George saw he was older than he had first thought, late forties at least. 'What about Isabelle Morny?' Both policemen were now staring past him, watching him and yet pretending not to. Is it really possible to tell a liar by his expression? Not that it mattered now, since he was telling the truth.

'I don't know,' he said. 'But about ten minutes later, Hammerson barged in and started insulting everyone, especially me . . .'

'Ten minutes or fifteen?' Dyle was scribbling over some typed notes.

George thought. 'Maybe nearer fifteen. I'd made myself some hot tea.'

'In this weather?' Dyle was smiling again.

'It all helps.'

'Let me see your hands.' Skipwith had walked over to him. George spread them out on the desk. He had thick muscular hands, though the long fingers were widely spaced, a legacy perhaps of stretching for the octaves. 'These are how you make your living?'

'They are.' And George was suddenly afraid. Afraid of this tubby sour-faced man, with his ferret nose and scant reddish hair.

'What are you after, Tod?' Dyle was looking from one to the other. They must both be about the same age, this urbane yet oddly unkempt pianist and the muscular Sergeant with so much anger pent up inside him. There were times when he was afraid of Skipwith himself.

The younger policeman turned away. 'Just interested,' he said. 'I had an idea.'

'Share it with me.' It was George now who was watching the other two, enjoying the temporary luxury of being a spectator.

'He'd need big gloves,' said Skipwith smoothly. 'That's all.' And he returned to his perch by the bookcase. 'Tell us more about Hammerson when he came in. How did he look?'

George nodded, to show he understood the significance of the question. 'Yes,' he said. 'One eye was very inflamed. At the time I thought he was just angry. I realize now that that was the result of Isabelle's poking him in the eye.'

'A spirited young lady,' said Dyle.

George grinned. 'She certainly is.' There was a stifled sound from Skipwith, a sort of liquid sizzling. 'A girl and a half,' George added, encouraged by his enemy's reaction.

'Remind us what he said.'

George rubbed one eye. 'He was on about ruining me.'

'That hardly seems necessary,' remarked Dyle.

'What do you mean?'

'We enjoyed reading your profit and loss figures,' sneered Skipwith. 'You must have been very worried at what he said.'

'I was.' What was the point of denying it?

'And what else?'

'I didn't really take it all in.'

'Come now, Mr Sinclair. You took it in very well. He accused Mr Brock of sending these poison-pen letters, didn't he?' Dyle held up a sheaf of three or four examples. 'They're poor stuff, but they could needle.'

'I didn't believe Rupert had anything to do with those.'

'Why not?'

'Poison-pen letters come from twisted inarticulate people. Rupert is all tongue.'

'Oh, yes?' Skipwith was coming over again.

'Yes.' George distinctly did not like having the squat man behind him.

'And what did he have to say about the egregious Mr Winston Wheeler?'

George furrowed his brow. 'He didn't. He just said he had a problem. Starting today.'

'He was rather well informed,' said Dyle.

'Bit of a clairvoyant,' chipped in Skipwith. 'We've discovered something rather interesting about Mr Wheeler, thanks to this investigation. Actually,' he licked his lips, 'it involves you too.'

'In that?'

'In that it's a serious offence to employ someone in this country who hasn't got a work permit.'

'But Winston's British,' protested George. 'He was born in Huddersfield.'

'So he was.' Skipwith was relishing his own words. 'Huddersfield, *Barbados*. He's only here on a student visa, isn't he? Or didn't he tell you that?'

'No, of course he didn't,' said George flatly. Winston without a work permit meant what? A large fine? And, what was far worse, no Leporello for the future shows. How could he afford to find a new bass, and pay for the rehearsals? Even assuming he wasn't in jail himself.

'So when this colourful scene was finished, did Hammerson leave?'

'Yes. He pushed past Jane.'

'Going through the Saloon door?'

'No, out into the corridor.'

'That's funny.' Skipwith's face held not the trace of a smile. 'You said Mrs Nuneham had gone into the Saloon to fetch some costumes. She wouldn't surely have gone through the guests in the Drawing Room? But then how did she get round to the other side?'

George sighed. 'She probably went round the outside of the house to take the things over to the washing

131

machine. I think she said it was in a room beyond the kitchen. There's another courtyard round there. Or she might have gone through the central courtyard for all I know. Ask her yourself.'

'We will.'

'And how long,' asked Dyle, pursuing his own idea, 'before Miss Morny came back and the second act started?'

'I don't know.'

'You don't know?' Skipwith was behind him again. If he touched him, George was ready. He bunched his fists.

'As pianist, I was first on, followed by the "beginners", Bruno and Winston, and then Jane. Isabelle wasn't due on stage for at least ten minutes.'

'So you didn't see her before the opera re-started?'

'No.'

'Even though you went back down to the kitchen yourself, didn't you?'

George held his head quite still. 'Did I? Oh, yes, I went back to have a pee.'

'In the room marked G for Gents?'

'No,' said George. 'There were several people milling about. I nipped down past the kitchen and found an old staff toilet at the end of that corridor. As a matter of fact, you can check my story with your new DNA tests.'

'How?' Skipwith had perched himself on the desk, frowning.

'Well,' said George, 'the thing wouldn't flush. If you nip along there smartish, with your police regulation teacup, and suck a sample from the bowl, that'll be genuine one hundred per cent proof Sinclair in there!' He grinned up at Skipwith. 'I suppose that's about where the division between senior and junior policemen lies?'

Skipwith stood up.

'Thank you,' said Dyle, standing up too. 'You've been

132

most helpful, Mr Sinclair. Will you nip across the corridor to the kitchen and ask Mrs Tregeare if she could join us?'

Thankful to be out of the room, George hurried across the corridor to find the kitchen full of people.

'Miss Cook has kindly walked over from Tredinnick to help me clear up,' Rose Bolitho was saying to an attentive Bruno. 'I can't tell you how much rubbish they left.'

'Mrs Tregeare! *Have* you seen my long screwdriver? The one I use to open the Flower Room cupboard. I always keep it on that shelf.'

Mrs Tregeare opened her mouth and then shut it again as Tom and Winston, arguing fiercely about some musical nicety, burst into the room.

'Hello, Mrs Bolitho!' Bruno rather fancied his manner with older women. 'May we forage for some sandwiches? We'd thought of walking along the cliffs and coming back along the shore.'

'You'll have to watch the tide,' said Mary Bolitho. 'It's very treacherous hereabouts.'

'You can say that again.' No one seemed to have noticed the slight yet still vivid, despite her neat black dress, figure of Eve Hammerson standing in the other doorway.

'My dear! What are you doing here?' Mary Bolitho rushed towards her.

'I had to have something to do. I wanted to help you all clear up.' Her brave smile had, like all her expressions, something indefinably dramatic about it. Even her mourning was shot silk.

'There was no need.' Alison Cook seemed to have abandoned any pretence of liking her late employer's wife. 'We can manage.'

'I know you can, my dear.' Now she was brisk Lady Bountiful, changing immediately into the Helpless Maiden. 'But I couldn't stay in that house, not *alone*, not *there*.'

'I'm afraid Tredinnick Hall *is* rather a forbidding house,' said Mary Bolitho, in a comforting tone. 'All alone on the cliffs.'

Deciding that he needed space, as in total seclusion, George slipped out as soon as he had delivered his message and hurried along the corridor. With his mind racing as it was now, nothing less than Beethoven, and Beethoven in great bleeding chunks, could assuage his inner turmoil. He was about to turn past the great staircase with its gloomy portraits and rank cloying smell of dead flowers when he heard raised voices from the landing above. Ed and Jane were having some sort of screaming match, and to his amazement he thought he heard Rupert joining in. He walked hurriedly on, turned left through the Tapestry Room and found himself, blessedly alone, in the Saloon.

All trace of the previous evening had already been erased. Whoever had removed the rows of gilt chairs had done so with speed and stealth. He had neither heard nor seen anything. Yet a hundred and fifty chairs had been spirited away. There was the piano, back in its original position in the tall bay window, and only the groaning gilt side tables, decked again with porcelain instead of last night's detritus of used glasses and programmes, punctuated the long spaces between the pillars against the wall.

Closing the door, he walked across to the piano, pulled up one of the tapestried chairs and launched himself, shoulders hunched, head well back, into the 'Prometheus Variations'. As the great chords shook the piano and the air, and as the whole room, heavy with the menace of the approaching storm, vibrated, from cornice to skirting, from floorboard to ceiling boss, with the concentrated essence of the music, a strange thing happened. It was as if the personality of Beethoven himself, confident and tentative, bombastic yet tender, dominant, domineering even, had escaped genie-like from some bottle encapsulated within that throbbing combination: the soaring piano and the manic figure pounding at its flying keys. Though well into the late B flat Sonata, with trills bouncing off the stucco carvings and discords dazzling the silent bronze mermaids, who writhed in perpetual yet unassuagable passion, George was himself aware of some brooding presence, though not a musical one.

Twice he turned, still playing, twice to scan an empty room. The frozen mermaids seemed to mock him, while, from the ceiling, bare sightless masks of careless cherubim blew empty trumpets in a blast of derision. And even as his music died away, stilled by his rising sense of panic, a thunderous cracking, like the splitting of some titanic oak, shocked him into total immobility.

'What . . .?'

Another crack, immediately overhead. Not overhead as in thunder, but overhead as in poised just feet above his fragile skull. It was shocking, invasive. He ducked, his hands covering his ringing ears. Another crack! And another! The chair fell as he ran from the piano, diving for the low door, and expecting, knowing even, that the roof was exploding, caving in. It was only when he reached the main stairs again, and met Rose coming down them with the light behind her, that his heart began to slow from its frightful pounding.

'What on earth's the matter?' She ran down the last few steps. 'Are you all right?'

He took her hand gratefully. 'I think so.'

'You look as if you've seen a ghost.'

He stared at her. 'I think . . .'

'Come and have a drink. Dad's installed himself in the Billiards Room. He's even found an electric fan!' She led him down the other corridor, past a row of strange stuffed mammals in domed glass cases. How could he tell her half the house must have fallen in? Especially when, in his head, he knew it hadn't. 'George needs a drink,' she announced brightly as her parents, caught unawares, turned sharply from apparently sharing a kiss.

'What?' The Colonel looked unexpectedly shy.

'He's seen a ghost.'

'Bloody rubbish!' The old soldier was in no mood for further drama.

'Oh, Dad! I often think there's a ghost here. And especially during storms. There's certainly someone there. Maybe Black Jack? Sometimes I dream the whole village is sailing out to sea, with the shrouds of his victims streaming away in the winds, propelling us all on to the Penpoltho Rocks.'

'Sounds very nice, dear,' said Mrs Bolitho, who had been half turned away from them, busy with her powder compact.

'Poetical claptrap!' grumbled her husband.

'No, it's not,' contradicted his wife. 'What were you saying last week about that voice in the Gun Room? That *must* have been a ghost.'

'*Nonsense!*' protested the Colonel, colouring ripely. 'What I said was, I got a feeling someone was trying to communicate with me. So I said out loud, feeling a perfect bloody fool, I can tell you, "I'm listening if you've anything you want to tell me." '

'And what happened?' asked George, his spine tingling again.

The Colonel paused to relight his pipe. 'That was the curious thing,' he said, between voluminous blue-grey puffs.

'Well?' prompted Rose, to whom this story was new.

'Well . . . I did think, though it was nothing really.'

'*What* was?' cried Rose, exasperated.

'It was like a breeze, a bit chilly, though.'

'You said it was a sigh,' said Mrs Bolitho.

The Colonel shrugged. 'A breeze. A sigh. What's the difference? I don't believe in ghosts.'

'Let's hear what happened to George,' said his wife again. She, too, had been shocked by her guest's pallor. She sat down and picked up the piece of tapestry she had been working on all summer.

The Colonel stared at his unwelcome guest. He hadn't wanted this man in his house at all. Since his arrival, he'd drunk the last bottle of the '78 Montrachet, a man had been done to death, on top of which Rose wanted to marry him, and now he was complaining about the house being haunted. Over the years, the Colonel had accumulated something of a track record with stares, of varying strengths and pungencies, depending on the circumstances. For George he uncorked his strongest vintage. With such a stare had he quelled the mad Maharajah of Javapore, last of the Red Moghuls, when the monarch had impudently threatened him with bloody disembowelment. With such a stare had he subdued the whirling dervish chieftain of the Sudanese delta when the less demanding solution of a pistol shot to the head (though richly deserved) would have ignited the whole of the Horn of Africa.

Rose blanched when she saw her father's face, and Mrs Bolitho quietly put down her tatting in case flight became necessary. But to George, lost in his own thoughts, the Colonel's swelling veins and bulging bloodshot eyeballs served only to excite his sympathy.

'I'm afraid this has been a dreadful strain on you,' he said, reaching over and patting the old man on his sleeve.

The Colonel, completely disarmed, sighed deeply. 'Yes,' he said, nodding his grey head with real feeling. 'Yes, it has.' And smiled. Mrs Bolitho and Rose just gaped.

'On the other hand,' said George, 'I'll tell you what *did* give me rather a turn. I thought the ceiling was coming down.'

The Colonel looked up sharply. 'The ceiling?'

'Yes. There was a sort of cracking sound, very loud, and more than once. As if the timbers had suddenly gone.'

'Do you think we'd better send for Saunders?' asked Mrs Bolitho, concerned.

'I must . . .' The Colonel had pulled himself out of his chair, and was moving towards the door. 'I'd better—'

'Do leave it to Saunders, dear,' called his wife after his retreating figure. 'Remember what happened to Archie! His friend,' she said, turning back to George. '*Would* try and fix his roof in London himself.'

'Was he hurt?' asked Rose vaguely.

'Don't be silly, darling. Those houses have five storeys and a basement. Dead as a dodo.'

Chapter Eighteen

'What are you doing?'

Rose had watched her father's face during George's description of what he had heard, and had seen the colour drain from those scarlet weather-beaten features she loved so well.

When the Colonel had risen, somewhat shakily, and stumbled away with his mumbled excuse, she had waited for a short while and then followed him. He was, as she had expected, seated at his desk, one half of it loaded with Chief Inspector Dyle's gadgetry.

He looked up and she almost gasped. He had aged ten years, his temples now sunken and his eyes so sad. Seeing her, he tried to smile and failed. 'If you must know...' even his voice sounded higher, less secure, '... I'm making my Will.'

'Not again!' The Colonel was rather prone to adding and subtracting codicils, depending on the state of his liver. She went over and laid her hand on his shoulder. 'Dearest Dad. You'd better tell me what the matter is.'

His great frame shook with a massive sigh, a sigh that seemed to encompass his whole being. Then he turned his head and looked up into her eyes, his eyes black and brooding, and nodded. 'Yes,' he said. 'You are the last of the Bolithos. You'd better know.'

She sat down on the edge of the desk. 'Dad, there

are hundreds of Bolithos all over Cornwall. Penzance positively pullulates with them.'

He shrugged. 'Not of our line. Not Bolitho of Bolitho. It rests with you now. That noise your friend heard—'

'The cracking? What he thought was the roof timbers giving way?

'Yes.'

'I myself have heard that sound twice.'

'And?' She was staring at him, mystified.

'Once when my father died, and once when your uncle Bevil died. It heralds the death of a Bolitho.'

'Oh, Dad! What nonsense!' Yet her back was chilled.

He shook his head sadly. 'I wish it were. But I already knew about the sound because my grandfather had told me. What a fine old man he was. I wish you could have known him.'

'I love his portrait.'

'It's a good likeness. His hair was so fine. He used to let me run my fingers through it when he sat by the fireside in the Oak Room. He told me about the cracking timbers. Each time for his poor sons. And it's said they could hear the roof cracking the other side of Tredinnick when they hanged the old Squire up at the crossroads.'

'I love this house,' she said suddenly. 'It's part of us, isn't it?'

'And will Mr Sinclair become part of us too?' he asked softly, his sad eyes fixed again on hers.

She smiled. 'I hope so. Oh, Dad! Don't say it. I know you think he's after my money.'

'There's a great deal of it, more than you might expect.'

She shook her head vigorously. 'He's not interested in that. I doubt if he's given it a thought.'

'Those of us who have money,' said her father drily, 'are apt to underestimate its importance to those who do not.'

'He's so clever,' she said, 'and so unassuming.'

'He may also be a murderer.'

'Never.'

'Be that as it may,' he said, picking up his pen again, 'it seems that I am to be the next victim, and I have one or two revisions to make to my Will.'

'Why you? Why not Mother?'

'Because,' said the Colonel grandly, 'your mother is not a Bolitho.'

'Or me?'

He opened a drawer and drew out a small polished automatic which smelled strongly of oil. 'I want you to keep this with you at all times. At least you know how to use it. My life is nearly done with, yours is just starting.'

'Dad!' But she took it, slipping it expertly into the pocket of her jeans. 'I hope I don't fulfil the prophecy by shooting myself in the bottom!'

He laughed. 'Sorry to be so melodramatic, darling. But the danger is real, or so I believe. Now, send me two of those singers who seem settled here for life. They can earn their supper by witnessing this for me.'

At the other end of the house, Mrs Tregeare, her fierce thin mouth set in a line of intransigent ill-humour, was using up much of her angry vigour in polishing the Colonel's great silver cup, the Oudipore Trophy, an exuberant example of the Indian silversmith's skill.

'To Second Lieutenant William Bevil Llewellyn Bolitho, of the Duke of Cornwall's Fusiliers. Winner of the 1938 Oudipore Pig-Sticking Prize. Presented by H.H. The Rajah of Oudipore.'

She could still remember him as he was then, a red-faced young subaltern with copious black hair, a shattering laugh, and an eager eye for the ladies. Mrs Tregeare, only a few years older, and married to a kind, if unimaginative, under-gardener, would gladly have accommodated the young soldier had his eye fallen upon her during his infrequent leaves home. But no, it had been that buxom bit of mischief Daisy Pinnock who'd introduced him to the joys of uninhibited sex among the shallows on Bolitho beach. Five years they'd cavorted all over the peninsula, pretending nobody knew, whereas *everyone* knew, except Bob Pinnock, of course. But then he, poor soul, was too simple to recognize his own reflection, and it was no surprise to anyone that he was one of the first casualties during the retreat to Dunkirk. Had there been a child? She was getting too old to remember anything these days . . .

She lifted her head. Not for nothing had she lived here for more than eighty summers. There was that in the air that told her the long-awaited storm was about to break. 'I'd best be off home,' she murmured to herself. 'I'm too old for another bout of pneumonia. I'll finish this tomorrow.'

Putting down the cup, and with it her memories, she crossed the kitchen to fetch her coat. Out in the darkness, also aware of the gathering storm, a figure watched with narrowed eyes, watched the old woman pattering across the kitchen, and then watched her returning again because she thought she had forgotten something. The watcher let out a hiss of impatience. If the rain came . . .

Mrs Tregeare, now wrapped in her coat, let herself out of the back door, locked it behind her, and walked across the yard and out through the stable archway. She had two routes home: east by the cliff path, or west down the drive. To the watcher's relief, she took the former, striding out with an unexpected turn of speed.

Down through the pines she went, and out along the cliff path, an honest woman, wracked with no malice, and bearing no grudges, an unquestioning Christian safe in her sure and certain hope of the Resurrection. When the blow came, a blow that splintered her old skull, driving fragments deep into her anguished brain, it was, perhaps, as sudden an end to a long life as she could reasonably have expected.

She dropped without a sound, her bony body seeming almost to sink in upon itself, so that, dead, there appeared that much less of her than there had been alive. The murderer bent over her corpse and, just to make sure, aimed a further two blows at her battered skull before rolling the body over the cliffside, and then hurrying away.

The coming of the storm an hour later, while dreaded by anyone out and about on or round the peninsula that night, such as the Tresillian family whose two elder sons were out on a fishing expedition, or DS Reynolds on sentry duty by the Bolitho entrance gates, was greeted, of course, with complete indifference by Mrs Tregeare's corpse, battered hither and thither among the foaming rocks at the foot of the cliff. But it came as welcome relief to all the humans stifling indoors, after four days of sultry temperatures and sweaty clothes. Most of all was it welcomed by those curious growths deep within Bolitho, the various fungi and related vegetation, whose very survival had been called into doubt by the prolonged heat and drought.

Nor was the storm alone in its enthusiastic generation of heat. George, returning from the bathroom, met Isabelle coming the other way and grasped her hand.

'I love you,' he said, throatily.

'That's good,' she said, with a laugh. 'Because I want you to give me away.'

'Give you away?' He was rubbing his hair vigorously with his towel. 'How do you mean?'

'In marriage. I'm going to marry Winston!'

'Marry? *Winston!*'

'Aiy-aiy-aiy! You're so quick. You never said you were a genius.' She was openly laughing at him. 'Here, let me.' She took the towel. 'It's the only way.'

'The only way?' He couldn't think straight at all.

'The only way to stop him being deported, *chéri*. Do you want a Leporello or don't you?'

'Not that badly.' He snatched back the towel. 'Not at that price.' Fuming, he traipsed gloomily back to his room. Winston! Married to Isabelle!

As the lightning cracked and split the skies, and as the thunderclaps shook the buildings, a cataract of water was hurled down upon the land, drenching everything in its path. Sometimes a bolt of lightning would plummet on to a lone tree, clothing it in a brief but glorious coat of seething electricity, splitting it from crown to roots, and leaving it behind, a blackened carcass. Sometimes it would light the whole panorama, bathing the shuddering landscape in an eerie blue phosphorescence, so that the details lost in the night would suddenly loom closer and more threatening than by day.

George, quite unable to sleep after Isabelle's contribution, watched, enthralled despite his misery, from his bedroom window, blissfully aghast at the savage power of nature. When the sheet lightning flared far out to sea, he could make out the rollers lit up through the usually impenetrable pines that straggled down beyond the lawn. As the storm bellowed in the chimney, and rattled at the window-panes, there was something both intimate and intimidating about its intrusive strength. Yet for centuries Man had dwelt on or near this spot, surviving in stone huts, mud huts, beneath plaited straw hurdles and, even earlier, in the caves beyond the Point, living out the primeval storms of history. And not only Man. If the newly discovered cave paintings at Bude were to be believed, centaurs also had colonized this coast, muscular horse–men, with silvery manes that must have flown on a night like this.

'It's wonderful, isn't it?'

He turned at the voice. Rose had crept in without his noticing. He nodded. After a bit, he said, 'I've always loved storms.'

'Me too.' She had placed her arms around his waist, laying her head against his back. 'Are you frightened?'

He turned round. She was looking up at him, her face pale and tense. 'Of the storm?' he asked.

She shook her head. 'Of the murderer.'

He shrugged. 'I doubt he'd be bothered with me.'

'What if it's a woman?'

'Running old Hammerson through with a sword? It's possible, I suppose. A bit, well, violent.'

She giggled. 'It wouldn't be easy to murder someone without violence.' She pulled out her gun. 'Look.'

He stared at it, open-mouthed. 'What are you doing with that?'

'My father gave it to me. He thinks either he or I is the next victim.'

'That's crazy!'

'It's because of what you said.'

'I don't understand.'

'The cracking timbers . . . remember?'

'*Remember?* I thought the whole lot was coming down on my head.' A brilliant burst of lightning lit the whole room, followed by a roar of thunder.

'Dad says that only happens when a Bolitho dies.'

'Every time?'

'There aren't that many of us.'

'Bit of a rare breed, eh?' He was smiling again.

'Actually there are only two left, Dad and me.'

'Well, you'd better get breeding!' He laughed.

'Precisely.' His smile died away in the face of her intense expression. 'Please, kiss me.' He did as he was told, and why not, in the circumstances? Shortly afterwards, he took her into the great oak bed, while the storm beat upon the house, and the seething waves carried Mrs Tregeare's body triumphantly out to sea.

Chapter Nineteen

When they woke, curled companionably together, it was still night, but the storm had passed. Outside, the trees dripped luxuriously, pattering the gleaming undergrowth with speckles of water. Inside the house, deep inside, water also dripped, sipping and sopping among the thirsty fungi, reinvigorating the thirsty growths.

'You're still alive,' he said.

'Mmm.' Rose stretched and yawned luxuriously. 'Have you got any Kleenex?'

George sighed and closed his eyes again. 'It's your house,' he said. 'You tell me.' He moved his head and felt something hard under the pillow. 'What's this?'

'My gun.'

'Your *gun*?'

'Just in case.'

'Just in case what?'

'In case you were a disciple of Pincette: "*embrasser pour mieux étrangler*".'

'What's that mean?' He was still half asleep.

'Hugging someone makes it easier to strangle them.' She giggled.

'Hugging . . .' He sat up abruptly, then gathered her to him, laughing. 'What a little optimist you are.'

'Just careful.'

'Do you think we ought to check on your father?'

'Why not!' She seemed immediately enthused by some atavistic taste for adventure. 'It shouldn't be difficult.' Pulling on some clothes, and holding her gun in a way that suggested professional familiarity, she led George, now in his dressing-gown, out into the darkened corridor.

'Where's your father sleep?'

'In the Oak Room. It's above the Billiards Room, overlooking the rose garden. This way.' She even had a torch!

Twice, as they made their way cautiously round the eerie corridors, they heard voices whispering in the dark, Isabelle and Maria, perhaps, or Jane with Ed or, more likely, with Winston. The white roundel of Rose's torchlight preceded them, illuminating the threadbare carpets and catching sudden reflections in the old cabinets and bookcases which lined the walls.

'It's a long way,' George was whispering as he eased open the door to the next corridor, when suddenly he gasped. Frighteningly, another sound had broken upon them, a harsh vibrating snarl that seemed impervious to the hushed solemnity of the night. 'God! What's that?'

Rose giggled. 'All's well,' she said.

'You mean . . .?' The noise was rising and falling. It was shockingly loud.

'That's my father snoring.'

'I've never heard anything like it!'

'At least he's alive.'

'How on earth does your mother sleep?'

'She has a pair of earmuffs. Proper gunnery ones. She wouldn't hear if the house fell down.'

'I see.'

She took his hand. 'Back to bed?'

He was still staring at the Colonel's bedroom door. 'Why not?'

Slowly they retraced their steps. As they passed one

of the bedroom doors, they heard a sudden soft cry and then a muffled voice through the darkness. '*Éventrez-moi! Éventrez-moi!*'

Rose had stopped, and turned to smile up at George, happy to celebrate another couple's fulfilment to match her own. But one glance at his face in the gloom, and she hurried on, fighting to subdue a pain that grew within her. And when, an hour later, his expression hidden by the darkness, George accepted further solace in her arms, at that same moment two young fishermen, their faces lashed white by the salty spray, were hauling in their latest catch. The battered and all but unrecognizable body of Mrs Tregeare.

When they woke a second time, it was light and someone was pounding on the door.

'What . . . What is it?' Thank God he'd locked it.

'Are you there?' A muffled voice. 'It's Ed. For God's sake come down.'

He grabbed his dressing-gown, ran to the door and unlocked it. 'What?'

'The daughter's disappeared! And they're saying the cook's been found drowned. There's bedlam downstairs, I thought I'd better . . .'

He'd caught sight of Rose, swathed in a sheet.

'Mrs Tregeare?' she said, oblivious of her appearance. '*Drowned?*'

Ed gulped. 'That's what the constable is saying,' he said, staring at her. 'The senior bods are down at the village now. Your father's out in the grounds with several men from the farm. They're in a right panic about you.'

'Oh, no!' Her eyes were full of tears. 'Poor Mrs Tregeare.'

'I'm so sorry,' said George, looking, and feeling, rather helpless.

'*There you are!*' Mrs Bolitho, her face white and strained, pushed past Ed. 'Thank God! We've been so worried.'

'Really, Mother.'

Mrs Bolitho, who had shown no apparent surprise at her daughter's compromising costume, gave her a warm hug. 'Have you heard about poor Mrs Tregeare?'

'Is it true?'

'I can't think they'd make it up.' Mother and daughter walked off down the corridor, leaving George and Ed staring at each other.

Chapter Twenty

While Dyle and Skipwith went through their interrogations again, and George distributed the cheques that he was by no means sure his bank would honour, Rose and her mother busied themselves with preparing lunch for themselves, the Colonel and their nine involuntary guests.

'Bruno's allergic to cheese, isn't he?' asked Mrs Bolitho from the depths of the larder. 'And suet, I think he said . . .'

'Yes. And Maria can't eat meat.'

'Why not?' Mary Bolitho was unused to guests with selective appetites.

'I *think*,' whispered Rose, 'that it's something to do with her teeth.'

'Her *teeth*?' demanded her mother, no respecter of whisperings. 'What's wrong with them?'

'I *think* they're getting a bit wobbly,' whispered Rose again, giggling.

'Oh?' Mary Bolitho's own teeth had their moments of wobbling, so she suddenly felt a little bit more sympathetic. 'Shall we do a tomato omelette with mashed potato and some of these carrots?'

'This cupboard's *filthy*,' protested Rose. 'Really, Mrs Tregeare wasn't very tidy, was she?'

'My dear,' said her mother. 'At least she did it all.

That's the important thing. Do you think she slipped?'

'Of course not. She knew that path backwards. I suppose,' Rose considered the problem with her head on one side, 'she might have had a stroke.'

'Can you wash these potatoes for me?'

'Chuck them over. Or could she have had a heart attack?'

'Don't be ridiculous,' said her mother, slicing some carrots with sudden vigour, 'she was only, what, eighty-four?'

Rose smiled at her mother. 'No age at all!'

'Exactly!'

'*Here* you are!' roared the Colonel, marching in from the corridor. 'I suppose you realize I had Weams and Sheepshanks dragging the mill pond until someone was kind enough to tell me you were entertaining our guests dressed in a *sheet!*' He shouted with laughter. 'What a girl!' He hugged her as well. 'I'd like to know where you kept the pistol!'

'Billy!' Mary Bolitho was always made uneasy by his boisterous way with their daughter.

'Is he going to marry you?'

'*Father!*' Even Rose was embarrassed by him.

'Shall I ask his intentions?'

'Do that and I'll make damned sure the prophecy comes true. Myself!' This time they both laughed. Mary Bolitho, watching them, with their matching dark looks and raffish smiles, felt a deep and highly uncharacteristic pang of jealousy. When had her husband, for all his gallantry, ever laughed with her like that?

'He's reading in the Billiards Room,' said the Colonel, more seriously. 'You can ask him – or I shall. I can't have loose gossip on the estate.'

'What estate?' countered Rose, half-angry again. 'A few hundred acres of scrub and sixty cottages more or less unfit for human habitation?'

'You or me?' It seemed the Colonel was serious.

'I'll go,' she said. 'But you can peel these potatoes. Done?'

'Done!' It was years since the Colonel had helped in the kitchen. It was almost an adventure for him, and he settled down with rather more enthusiasm than Rose felt for her own errand.

George was, indeed, reading in the Billiards Room, sprawled in the red leather wing-chair, while Rupert lay snoring on the sofa underneath the window. She crossed to where George sat, and knelt beside him.

'Well?' He smiled down at her, wary.

'My father wants to know your intentions.'

'You mean . . .?'

'He's heard about last night. He wants to know if you mean to marry me!' She laughed to try to take what she knew he would see as the silliness out of the question. 'He's very old-fashioned.'

George stared at her. 'It's early days,' he said at last. 'Don't you feel that?'

Her mouth tasted bitter. 'Of course I do. But I do love you, you know that.'

He leant down to kiss her hair. What is such an avowal if not often an invitation for the echo? Surely she could not expect so much from him after a single night?

'You're very lovely,' he said, temporizing.

'He's so old, you see,' she said. 'He's worried about the money.' She couldn't look at him. She might even have had trouble looking at herself. Was she really trying to buy herself a husband?

'What money?' He sounded genuinely puzzled.

'Well, mine, of course. I know it wouldn't make any difference,' she said, 'but being an only child, I have rather a lot.'

'I'd have thought it was the other way round,' said

George thoughtfully. 'If you've got lots of money, I'd have thought he'd want to steer you clear of people like me.'

This time she did look at him. 'People like you?'

'Yes! Fortune-hunters, impecunious pianists with eight singers and a lorry to support!'

'Murderers even!' she said and her laugh sounded half cracked.

At least he laughed too. 'There you are!' he said triumphantly.

'Doesn't the idea appeal at all?'

'Marry? Live down here? What would I do?'

'Do? There's masses to do. You could help me run the estate—'

'Great! What does that entail? Chatting up the tenants? Teasing the bull?'

'Don't be silly. And you can take Daddy's place on some of his committees. He's President of the British Legion.'

'Well, you can forget that! I've never even seen a desert.'

'That's the French, you fool. These are old soldiers.'

'Oh? Well, I was in the Boy Scouts.'

'Not as often as little me,' murmured Rupert, waking up.

'Please be serious, George,' said Rose, ignoring him. 'You'd be wonderful.'

'Mr Sinclair?' It was Skipwith, at his most menacing. 'A word if you please.'

'In the Library?'

'If you would.' The accompanying gesture left no room for debate. Hiding his relief at escaping Rose's intense interrogation he followed the squat detective back down the corridor to where Dyle sat waiting for him, recorder at the ready.

'Did you go out last night, sir?'

'Certainly not! There was a colossal storm.'

Dyle smiled. 'We have a report that Miss Morny was seen drying your hair with a towel.'

George shrugged. 'That's right.'

'How did you get it wet?'

'I washed it. In the bath.'

Skipwith consulted a piece of paper. 'You have a hair-dryer in your bedroom,' he said.

'That's right,' said George. 'I was going back there, when I met Isabelle.'

'You definitely deny going out of the house last night?'

'Definitely,' said George. 'One hundred per cent.'

Dyle stretched his legs and clasped his hands behind his neck. 'I'd like to go back to when you first met Mr Hammerson . . .'

And they were still at it when Rose put her head round the door to say that George was wanted for lunch.

'How's it going?' she asked him as soon as Dyle, with slight reluctance, had allowed him to leave.

'Nothing new,' he said wearily. 'I can't tell them what I don't know.'

'Do they think Mrs Tregeare was murdered?'

He stared straight ahead. 'I don't think they know,' he said slowly. 'But if they do, they aren't saying. I expect there'll be an autopsy and then we'll all know.' After that, they walked on in silence.

When they reached the Saloon, where the Colonel had managed to set up lunch on a series of card tables, George found an envelope addressed to him on his chair.

'What's this?' he said, picking it up.

'Delivered this morning,' grunted the Colonel, who was busy wrestling with the mashed potatoes. 'On the kitchen window-sill.'

With everyone watching, George opened the envelope. Inside it was a single sheet of paper on which, carefully cut and pasted, was the message:

I saw you.

'Anything interesting?' asked Mrs Bolitho brightly.

George looked up with a smile. 'Very dull,' he drawled, and put it in his pocket.

Chapter Twenty-One

That Monday morning proved a busy one for Dyle and Skipwith. First came the news of Mrs Tregeare's death, and subsequently the preliminary (and inconclusive) inspection of what was left of her. No sooner had they been driven back up to the house than a Bude solicitor, Roger Bullivant of Bullivant, Trelawney and Rees, had arrived with what purported to be Mr Hammerson's Last Will and Testament, a document he had already presented to Mrs Hammerson at Tredinnick House. Indeed it was at her insistence that he had gone straight round to Bolitho Court.

'That complicates things,' murmured Skipwith, as they digested its contents.

'Or makes them very simple,' said Dyle. 'I suppose there's no doubt that this is genuine?'

'I drew it up myself,' said Bullivant, a plump man, in his thirties, with sparse black hair and protuberant blue eyes. 'We do most of what I'd call the "county" work round here.'

'Including the Bolithos?'

The solicitor inclined his head. 'We do a great deal of business for the Bolitho family,' he said. 'Not only the Bolithos of Bolitho, of course, but also the Bolithos of Bickstead Hall, and the Bolithos formerly of Bude Manor, now of 136c, Bath Road, Exeter.'

'I see.'

'Mrs Hammerson was very upset by the last bequest.'

'Is it a large proportion of the estate?'

Bullivant folded his hands together. 'I really wouldn't know,' he said. 'I'd never met Mr Hammerson before last Thursday. Although,' he added, 'I should hazard the guess that it was not. He paid close to eight hundred thousand pounds for Tredinnick Hall and its dependencies, and I do know there was no mortgage involved.'

'You acted for the vendors?'

Again the legal head was inclined. 'The late Mrs Tredinnick's family are one of our oldest clients,' he said. 'The sale of the house was a grave blow to them. Although they were pleased with the price.'

'I see that you are named co-executor with Mr Alan Peascod Waterhouse. He is ... Mr Hammerson's business partner?'

'Perhaps.' Bullivant seemed disinclined to commit himself. 'I've never met the gentleman.'

Dyle rose. 'Thank you for such prompt help,' he said. 'I shall want to see Mrs Hammerson and Mr Waterhouse as soon as possible. If you're going back ...?'

Bullivant nodded. 'I'll give them the message.'

'And the secretary, Miss Cook.'

'As you wish.'

When the solicitor had left, the two policemen stared at each other.

'Well!' Skipwith wiped his mouth. 'I didn't expect that.'

Dyle smiled. 'Let's wait to get some more background. Ring Doc Smithers and say we really need his best guess about Mrs T as soon as he can.'

'Do you think it's coincidence?' Skipwith watched his chief carefully.

'Murder,' said Dyle. 'No doubt about it, though we

may never prove it after a night in that sea. By the way, Reynolds found a drawer with seventeen and a half pairs of gloves in the hall. Every conceivable size. Anyone could have helped themselves.'

The first person to arrive was Waterhouse, a giant of a man, with thick grey eyebrows and even thicker red lips. He was wearing a loose grey suit that smelt of tobacco.

'How would you describe your relationship with Mr Hammerson?'

The big man lounged back in his chair, which gave a warning creak. 'May I smoke?'

Dyle smiled and made a note. 'Please do,' he said. 'This is private property.'

Waterhouse stared at him, then pulled out a battered brown cigar and set about igniting it. 'Clay Hammerson and I,' he said, between pungent puffs of speckled smoke, 'did quite a bit of business on the side. He was senior partner for Beeston Lefevre in London. They're a major investment bank based in New York.'

'Thank you,' said Dyle, with just a trace of irony. 'And what sort of work are you in?'

Waterhouse twinkled. 'Information,' he said, with what might have been intended as a charming self-deprecatory grin. 'Always have been. Man and boy.'

'Except,' said Dyle smoothly, 'when you were involved with Burkedale Investments.'

Waterhouse shrugged. 'I knew you'd turn that up.'

'Six years you got.'

'Reduced to five on appeal. I spent most of it at Ford. A picnic.' He chuckled. 'But I shan't be going back. What I do is quite legal. Sometimes I even help your people. We'd just found out about that nigger, for instance, and Clay had already dictated a letter about

159

one of the other entertainers . . .' He felt in his pocket and produced a sheet of paper.

Dyle waved it aside. 'Tell me more about what you actually did together.'

'Information. As I said. Clay was an info freak. He needed to know everything about everyone. And paid very handsomely.'

'Through the bank?'

'Depended on the info,' said Waterhouse, suddenly looking cautious. 'He was very precise about paying himself for local stuff.'

'Local stuff?'

Waterhouse's eyes gleamed. He leant forward. 'Yes,' he said. 'Like about the Colonel here. They had a frightful row before the opera. Clay loved it. He said he'd really got the old geezer puffing and blowing.'

'It's the first we've heard about it.'

'You ask the old buffer.' Waterhouse had wrinkled his nose. 'Thinks he's so right and proper. You ask him about his son and heir.' He tapped his nose in a knowing gesture.

'What would you estimate as the likely size of Mr Hammerson's estate, approximately?'

Waterhouse had regained his twinkle. 'Between ten and fifteen million. Pounds that is. Probably more. I know his bonus was over two million last year, and a man like him doesn't pay much tax.' He simpered. 'I'll miss him.'

'You know that you're an executor of his Will?'

The big man grinned. 'That'll keep me busy for a few months.'

'What can you tell us about his wife?'

'Eve?' He threw back his head and laughed coarsely. 'A long-suffering lady. But then she got a hundred thousand a year to spend. So she didn't make too many waves.'

160

'He had affairs?'

'He always had something on the go. Liked them small and energetic.'

'Did you like him?'

Waterhouse returned the Chief Inspector's stare. 'I like anyone who gives me as much business as Clay did. A really good mucker too. I'll miss him.'

Yet Mrs Hammerson, when she finally arrived, gave a rather different portrayal of her husband's life.

'I've always assumed,' she said, 'that that frightful man had some hold over him. Clay hated him, but put up with him for whatever reason.'

'Perhaps because he was useful?'

'*Useful?*' The idea was clearly a new one to her.

'Yes. Providing information.'

She considered the point. 'Clay certainly did like knowing about people. But it was more for the gossip angle than for serious business. After all, his business was largely investment in major corporations.'

'Mergers? Takeovers?'

'Those too, of course. Oh, I see what you mean. He might have used Alan for that. Perhaps he did.' She shrugged. 'But he hated him.'

'He made him an executor of the Will.'

She laughed. 'He was always re-making his Will. God knows he didn't expect to die. Or at least not like that. He used to say it was cheaper to make Alan an executor, as he couldn't claim the sort of fees an accountant or an attorney could charge.'

'Were you aware of the terms of the Will?'

She arched her eyebrows. 'You mean the final bequest?' She laughed. A surprisingly hoarse sound. 'There was always one of those around. He was an important financier. Lots of testosterone sloshing about. He needed an accommodating receptacle to dump it in. I understood that. Rather them than me in the middle of the afternoon!' Her smile was too humorous to be false.

'No hard feelings between you?'

She shook her head. 'Certainly not. You'll have noticed that I'm very much the main beneficiary. And he knew I had friends.'

'Lovers?'

She gazed at him steadily. 'Of course,' she said. 'I'm only thirty-eight. I enjoy it as much as I expect you both do.' She gave them both a defiant smile. 'No problem there, I assure you!'

As for Alison Cook, the murdered man's secretary, she concurred with Mrs Hammerson. Asked about Waterhouse, she wrinkled her delicate nose. 'Not a very nice man,' was her cautious judgement. 'Mr Hammerson detested him, but he did produce the goods.'

'Privately or for Beeston Lefevre?'

She smiled. 'Both. But Mr Hammerson was very careful to differentiate between the two. He knew that Mr Waterhouse had been to prison, and that he would be open to attack from within the firm if anyone started throwing mud. The major enquiry work was done by a firm called Trinity and Samson, but sometimes he said we needed a more down-to-earth approach.'

'He said?'

'Mr Hammerson, that is.'

'Tell us where you fit in?' Skipwith was back against the bookcase, eyeing her with a supercilious expression. 'You're the secretary, right?'

She smiled at him. 'I have the same sort of job as you do, Sergeant,' she said sweetly, 'except I'm on thirty-three thousand a year, plus a guaranteed bonus, a Porsche and an index-linked pension. If it suits you to call me a secretary, I can afford to live with that.'

Skipwith scowled at her. 'It's what *he* called you.'

She shrugged. 'Mr Hammerson was the archetypal male chauvinist employer.'

Dyle gave her an appraising look. 'One of my constables said you were in tears that night he was killed.'

She nodded. 'I was fonder of him than I'd thought. He was . . . exciting to work with. He pulled off some very dramatic deals in the City.' She was wagging her head, as if insisting they believed her.

'You helped organize the opera evening here?'

'Yes Mr Hammerson saw them at some performance he went to in or near London. He evidently liked what he saw,' neither her face nor her voice held the slightest hint to suggest that his interest had been in anything but the music, 'so he asked me to help organize a performance they were giving near Taunton which he helped to pay for, and subsequently this performance here where he had quite a few corporate guests among the audience.'

'You've heard the terms of the Will?'

She laughed. 'I certainly have!'

'Did they surprise you?'

She shook her head. 'He made several similar bequests in the past. All since cancelled.'

'How do you know?'

'Because I typed most of them up for him.'

'Not this one?'

'No. I was in Frankfurt earlier in the week. Perhaps that's why he went to a local lawyer.'

'Are there copies of the earlier Wills?'

She frowned. 'There *may* be, but I doubt it. He was very keen on shredding all unwanted documents. Spying is very common in this business.'

'Hence Mr Waterhouse?' said Dyle.

She grinned. 'Precisely.'

'Do you like Mrs Hammerson?' enquired Skipwith.

She screwed her eyes up, staring past him. 'No,' she said, firmly. 'No, I don't.'

'Because?'

'Because she took his money, and squandered it on toy boys.' It was said in an entirely matter-of-fact way.

'And you, Miss Cook? Did you sleep with him too?' This from Dyle, accompanied with a sympathetic smile.

'No fear!' she said robustly. 'Not that he asked me. Absolutely against Company rules. The best sex in the world wouldn't make up for losing my job, or his for that matter.' She looked Dyle straight in the eyes. 'Is there anything else?' she enquired.

'Not for the moment, Miss Cook. Would you ask Miss Morny to join me here?'

'Certainly, Chief Inspector.'

They watched her trim behind leaving the room, carried on those spectacular legs. 'They'd have to pay me a big whack to stop me trying my luck there,' said Skipwith, licking his lips.

Dyle grinned. 'It's not what they'd pay you,' he said. 'It's what they'd pay her that would interest that little number!' He'd rather taken a fancy to her himself. There was a trim muscularity about her that might – *must* – bode well in bed.

When she entered, Isabelle gave off instead the unmistakable aura of damsel-in-distress. Her fragility, her creamy pallor, her large and liquid eyes, of palest cornflower, made her almost a caricature. If it was a performance, it was a very fine one.

'You have some more questions for me, Chief Inspecteur?'

'If I may. The one thing I don't understand from the autopsy is how Mr Hammerson broke his index finger in three places . . .'

'Oh!' cried Isabelle, opening her eyes very wide indeed. 'I expect that was me.'

'You?' Skipwith was staring at her hungrily.

'Yes. After I'd back-kicked him in the balls, and then poked his eye, he fell on the floor. I was just leaving when . . .'

164

'When . . .' Skipwith, poor man, was all too conscious of his own balls.

'When he said something rude.' She giggled and then pushed out her lips in a pout.

'And . . .' The suspense was killing them.

'And so! I went back and stamped on his fingers. *Comme ça!*' She lifted one shapely leg high above her waist and, bringing her heel down with a terrific crack, she ground it viciously into the carpet.

The two men stared at her. 'Thank you,' said Dyle, after a pause. 'That would seem to explain the multiple fracture.' She turned to leave, agreeably conscious of their eyes upon her. It was all she could do not to wiggle her bottom at them. 'One other thing, Miss Morny.' Dyle's voice had suddenly hardened. 'Were you aware of the terms of Mr Hammerson's Will?'

'His Will?' She had turned and was facing them, a sudden eagerness in her expression. 'You don't mean he did it?'

'Did what?'

'Well, Inspecteur, *Chief* Inspecteur,' she parted her lips in a beguiling little smile, 'you surely know that Mr Hammerson wanted to fuck me?'

Dyle nodded, unblinking. Skipwith's throat had gone painfully dry. He tried not to cough and ended by emitting a shrill little splutter. Isabelle smiled. '*So.* He was promising this, and promising that. Like men do.' She lowered one eyelid in Dyle's direction.

'You didn't . . .?' Skipwith's voice was hardly more than a squeak.

'Pay much attention? No, of course not.'

'No,' said Skipwith, louder. 'You didn't . . .?'

'Didn't what?' Could she really have misunderstood him?

'Let him . . . er . . .?'

'What my sergeant is anxious to ascertain,' explained

Dyle with a dry smile, 'is whether you and Mr Hammerson went to bed together.'

'Oh-la-la!' She hooted with laughter. 'But, of course not. With that awful man? *Jamais!*'

'He left you one hundred thousand pounds,' said Dyle.

'Free of estate duty,' chimed in Skipwith. Both men were now watching her intently.

She clapped her hands together. '*Bravo!* That is wonderful. When will they pay?' It was impossible to believe that she could see the implications, the sudden arrival of motive with a capital M to someone who already had both opportunity and ready access to the murder weapon. 'What a splendid joke!'

After she'd gone, they settled down to sift their data. 'What a wildcat!' said Skipwith, wiping his mouth. Dyle looked up and nodded. 'You didn't ask her about the other abrasion. The one on the forehead?'

Dyle shook his head again. 'I think we'll keep that to ourselves, just for the moment. Now let's deal with Colonel Blimp.'

As they expected, Colonel Bolitho settled himself down in his own Library with every sign of perfect assurance. 'Any luck, you fellows?' he asked, as if he had requested their presence as opposed to the other way round.

'Not as yet, sir,' said Dyle politely.

'Any news on Deirdre Tregeare?' He pulled a red spotted handkerchief out of his jacket sleeve and trumpeted loudly into it with his nose, before carrying out a prolonged rubbing and wiping during which his face was almost completely invisible. The two policemen watched without expression. 'Poor old girl.'

'I'm trying to get an idea of Mr Hammerson's relations with the rest of the household,' began Dyle cautiously.

'Quite right,' said the Colonel. 'No time spent on reconnaissance is ever wasted. That's what my old platoon commander taught me. Always kept that at the forefront. Of my mind, that is.'

'Quite so,' said Dyle soothingly. 'How, for example, did you and he get on?'

He suddenly got an unexpected glimpse of a very different man. The Colonel, like Isabelle, might enjoy playing a part, might indeed have played it for years with dogged persistence and without the need for overt applause. This Dyle could understand, since both he and Skipwith were often called upon to play a variety of parts in the cause of justice. But in the glance he received from the man opposite him there was so much plain humanity, so much simple honesty, that he was momentarily taken aback.

'You've heard,' said the Colonel flatly.

'Just gossip,' said Dyle, spreading out his hands as if to placate the old man. Skipwith, embarrassed, turned abruptly to stare out of the window. Himself the son of a boatman in Bude, the Colonel was to him an object of affectionate respect and a little kindly derision. He couldn't bear to hear what he thought was coming next.

'It was years ago,' said the Colonel. 'Before the war. I had a girl here. Married, I'm afraid, but that's neither here nor there now. She conceived a child and told me it was mine. I expect it was. We certainly tried hard enough.' He paused to wipe his eyes. 'She lost it, of course. Poor little mite.'

'A boy?' Dyle's voice was very soft.

'Dear little chap. I never saw him. There was enough scandal as it was. I don't know how that swine got hold of the story. He'd got it back to front – *typical*! Thought the boy was alive, and could cut Rose out. Thought himself so cocksure!' he barked, no other word for it.

'What did you say?'

'*Say?*' The Colonel was almost back in his traditional role. 'To that slimy shit? Not a word. *Not a word!* I walked away and left him.'

'Someone said they heard you shouting.'

'They certainly did,' said the Colonel with satisfaction. 'I was shouting at my wife, demanding to know why she'd let a damned great greasy turd into my house! Right in front of him, just in case he wasn't sure what I thought of him. But speak to him? Never again, I assure you of that, young man. Not in this life.'

'One more question, sir.'

'If you must.'

'If your son had lived, would it have affected Miss Rose Bolitho's inheritance?'

'Not a jot,' said the Colonel. 'My father left me a life-interest with remainder to my legitimate children. Naturally I've resigned most of my interest ... to help with inheritance, you see.' The two policemen were listening blankly. 'Of course I'd have left the boy something. I've nothing against bastards. Quite the reverse. The Squire's father came from the wrong side of the blanket, and so did the Leicestershire estate. There's been quite a lot of it in our family. But Rose is the proper heiress. Half a dozen bastards popping up now wouldn't alter that.'

'Is that likely?' asked Dyle with a slight grin.

The Colonel shook his head. 'Not half a dozen anyway!' He shouted with laughter, safely back now in his adopted lifetime role.

'At any rate, you didn't kill him?'

The Colonel's laughter paused, then redoubled. 'God, no!' he wheezed. 'Though now you mention it, I rather wish I had.'

Chapter Twenty-Two

'Have you seen this?' George was wandering in a half-dream through the shrubbery when Jane ran up clutching a tabloid newspaper, the *London Advertiser*.

LOVE BLOSSOMS IN
MURDER MANSION

ran the headline, and beneath it sat a blurred but very recognizable photograph of Winston kissing Isabelle while both smiled sideways at the camera. It must have been taken roughly where they were standing now.

> We are pleased to announce the engagement of Mr Winston Wheeler, the celebrated bass baritone from Huddersfield, Barbados, to Miss Isabelle Morny, the beautiful young soprano from Wyndham Mansions, W14.
>
> Among the stately showrooms of millionaire's residence, Bolitho Court, these two young artistes have learned to love each other while bloody murder stalks the corridors.
>
> Home of eccentric Bristol property magnate 'Colonel' William Bolithoe, an elderly bachelor with a mania for music, a visit by an opera group has seen first the murder of another millionaire, US banker

Clay Hammerson, now followed, unbelievably, by the mysterious death of the cook, Mrs Deirdre Tregeare, 93, of 16, Court Close, Bolitho.

The Devon & Cornwall police, led by Detective Chief Inspector Philip Dyle, anticipate an early arrest, failing which *The Advertiser* strongly recommends the immediate despatch of Hercule Poirot and Sherlock Holmes to clean up the Country House set!

'How unfunny,' said George, looking past Jane to avoid letting her misery add to his own. 'And illiterate.'

'Can't you do something about it?'

'Me?' Did she expect him to confess?

'She loves you?'

He snorted. 'Nonsense.'

'How do you know?'

'I heard them at it last night.'

She bowed her head. 'So did I.' She sniffed. 'But I made love to poor Ed later, so perhaps I shouldn't complain.'

George chuckled. 'I went to bed with our hostess,' he said. 'So I'm in the same boat.'

'You couldn't have!'

'Why not?'

'She's hideous!'

'Don't be absurd. She's got a lovely figure.'

'*Mrs Bolitho?*'

'Jane! Don't be ridiculous. *Rose* Bolitho.'

'I was going to say . . .'

'Still, if that's what Isabelle wants . . .'

'It *isn't*,' shouted Jane. 'Why won't you listen? She wants you. She told Winston you called it off. She's heartbroken. That's why she's helping him.'

'Not too heartbroken to fuck his socks off!'

Jane stamped her foot. 'Winston would fuck with anything that moved. Especially if it'll keep him in the UK.'

'Doesn't that upset you?'

'What do you think these are?' she demanded. Tears were inching down her chin. 'Do you think I walk round all day with a fucking *onion*, just to get a bit of sympathy?'

'So what should we do?'

'*Take her back!*' Jane was nearly hoarse with frustration. 'Get out of our hostess's knickers and get back where you belong!'

'You don't understand,' said George. 'She's—'

'Very beautiful. That's what she is. And she'd be a far better wife to you than Maria. What you saw in that old bag I'll never know. I remember saying to Ed . . .'

But before this fruitful reminiscence could continue, they met a team of policemen, shuffling towards them in a close line, all peering at the ground, which they were turning over with pointed sticks.

'Go back to the house, both of you, please.' It was Detective Sergeant Skipwith, and his expression was very grim.

'What's happened?' asked Jane.

'They already know at the house,' he replied, 'so there's no harm in telling you. Mrs Tregeare was definitely murdered. With a croquet mallet. Before being thrown in the sea.'

'Good Lord!'

'Yes,' said the policeman bitterly. 'And when we find the evidence, the man who did this will regret hurting a defenceless old lady like her.'

Without replying, George turned and walked back up the slope. Jane followed close behind him. Skirting the verandah, they could see, through the Dining Room windows, the four police clerks tapping away at their computers, painstakingly collating and cross-referencing all the minutiae of the investigation. The old woman in slacks seemed in control of distribution, limping from desk to desk, handing out and taking back sheaves of thin white paper while her villainous-looking assistant, a swarthy man with a pronounced squint, glowered at the world from behind a bank of silent telephones.

There was a pair of french windows at the corner of the building, leading to the servery for the Dining Room, and they let themselves in there and crossed the corridor to the kitchen in search of some coffee.

'I think that's a wonderful idea,' they heard someone saying. 'Wonderful.'

'What is?' asked Jane, walking straight up to Winston who was shovelling sugar into a small cup of something steaming. The room was full of people, the troupe, Rose, her mother.

'Mrs Hammerson here,' she was standing by the sink, 'has suggested that while we're marooned here, we might put on a show for the schoolchildren.'

'It's just a thought.' Mrs Hammerson smiled modestly. 'The children would love it so.'

Bruno cleared his throat. 'It's a nice idea but—'

'But?' Maria glared at him. 'But what?'

He shrugged. 'It's my larynx. I think it's relaxed.'

'So what?' Rupert slammed his mug down on the table. 'My larynx is so relaxed it's like a bit of old knicker elastic. That doesn't mean we couldn't do a show for the kids.'

'*And* I'm having trouble connecting with my support,' persisted Bruno, unwilling to back down.

Jane grabbed him by the jaw. 'Calling Support! Come in Support!' she shouted down his throat. Then she mimed listening by bending her ear towards him. 'Yes!' she said. 'I've made contact! Support's coming through loud and clear.'

'Very funny!' Bruno broke away from her. 'I've got nothing against a show for children. We just need to discuss fees, that's all.'

'*Fees!*' shouted Winston. 'We're talking about school-children here.'

'And I'm talking about mortgages, gas bills and my singing coach,' said Bruno. 'If you tell me the teachers work for free, and the caretaker, and the school secretary, then I'll sing for free too. Until then . . .'

'My wife . . .' began Winston.

'Your *what*?' asked George quietly.

'His wife,' replied Isabelle. 'As I hope to be very shortly.'

'No, you don't!' said George.

'Yes, I do.'

'*Isabelle!*'

'I do!' She was pouting again.

'I forbid it.'

'How *dare* you?' The room had gone quiet.

'Because.'

'*Because?* What sort of grammar is that?'

'Don't bandy grammar with me, Isabelle. I'm just telling you, that's all.'

There was a loud smack as she slapped his face. 'That for telling,' she said, 'and *that* for being unfaithful with that creature there!' She had slapped his face again, even harder.

'What about *you*?' he bellowed, grabbing her arms and forcing them behind her back, so that he was holding her, panting, against his chest. '*Éventrez-moi*, indeed!'

She laughed, right in his face.

'You've no right to talk to the lady like this.' Winston had stepped forward, his face working with some emotion, embarrassment, perhaps, or pride.

'I've every right,' shouted George. 'I'm all she's got to look after her.'

'An ex-lover?' scoffed Bruno.

'No,' shouted George. 'I'm her elder brother!'

The silence that fell was profound. Gradually the

173

hissing of a kettle began to reassure those watching that the world had not come to a complete end.

'Well!' said Mrs Bolitho, untying her apron. She opened her mouth to say more, but for the first time in her life she felt unable to utter a single word. Rose, staring at George, felt a sudden lessening of the oppressive gloom which had occupied her for the past hours. George was Isabelle's *brother*. Therefore ... She smiled. 'Has anyone seen Tino?' she said. 'There was a telephone call for him earlier. From his agent. It's sort of urgent. I quite forgot.'

'Checking he's still alive, I imagine,' murmured Rupert. 'I believe they do that once a year.' Maria giggled.

'If they mean the fat one,' whispered Mrs Hammerson to Alison Cook, 'I think I saw him poking about at the end of the kitchen corridor.'

'I'll go,' said George, unable to meet anyone's gaze. He was only too thankful to get out of the room. The kitchen corridor consisted of a U-shaped run, lined with bare shelving, round a mossy service court. 'Tino! *Tino!*' The doors still bore their enamel plaques, discreetly announcing 'Scullery', 'Still Room', 'Larder', and 'Lamps'. These four were all empty.

Round the corner was 'Boots', empty, 'Coals', empty, and then, at the far end 'Engine Room'. '*Tino!* Telephone call!' Here the door was ajar, and creaked horribly when he pushed it open. There was a strange smell and, suddenly frightened, he stepped forward and switched on the light. He had found Tino, or rather Tim, but he stood there without saying a word. For he was looking down at Tim. Not the Tim he knew, but a Tim with a black congested face, a Tim wearing nothing except a length of telephone cord twisted tight round his throat.

Chapter Twenty-Three

'They've arrested George!' Rose had burst into the Billiards Room where her mother and father were standing by the fireplace, talking in hushed voices to a thick-set man in a musty tweed suit.

'I'm afraid that was inevitable,' he said, with a quiet smile. 'That's why I'm here. I don't expect you remember me. I'm Roger Bullivant, of Bullivant, Trelawney and Rees. We acted for you when you bought the London flat. We must act, and swiftly.' He looked just as dynamic as a dead halibut.

'I remember,' she said flatly. What she remembered was a plodding pompous rigmarole made out of what could have been a very simple transaction. How could this absurd man help George now?

He must have read the scepticism in her expression, because his smile faded. 'Unfortunately he's agreed to talk to them despite, I'm quite sure, being advised of his rights. He'd have done much better to have stayed silent until I'd had a chance to hear his story.'

'I suppose,' said Rose acidly, 'he felt that, being innocent, he had nothing to hide.'

'Oh, quite.' Bullivant smirked. 'But it is tricky. Him finding both bodies, I mean.'

The Colonel nodded. 'I thought that,' he said. 'In

fact . . .' His voice trailed away when he saw his daughter's expression.

Meanwhile, in the Library, Skipwith was positively grinning with triumph.

'Do you know what the statistics are for people who find the corpse?' he said, thrusting his face at George.

'No,' said George wearily. This had been going on for nearly an hour.

'Twenty-eight per cent!' said Skipwith. '*Twenty-eight effing per cent!*'

'Twenty-eight per cent what?' George asked, even though he reckoned he could guess the answer.

'Did it, that's what!' The Sergeant's face was sweating with excitement. 'But you weren't content with finding one body. Oh no! That'd be too easy. You had to find *two* bodies, didn't you? There are no statistics for that.'

'If I'd known it would make such a difference, I'd have swum out to find Mrs Tregeare for you as well,' said George, unwisely.

Skipwith pounced. 'So you *do* admit to being out on the headland in the storm?'

'No. I've told you. I stayed indoors. I washed my hair. I went to bed.'

'You know . . .' Chief Inspector Dyle was sucking his pen thoughtfully. 'It is a bit awkward about your sister.' His face held kindly solicitude.

'I've explained,' said George. 'We didn't know we were related.'

'Incest isn't something the courts like,' snarled Skipwith. 'Not hereabouts.'

'I thought it was quite common in Cornwall,' said George.

'You—'

'Tod!' Dyle was tired too. 'Let's concentrate on Timothy Grant, as I believe you've told us the deceased was correctly named.'

'Yes.'

'We found this slip of paper in your coat pocket.'

'So I understand.'

'It reads: "I saw you".' Dyle's eyes were a light grey, with large mottled pupils, the lines on either side of his nose even more pronounced.

'I know.'

'What did you take that to mean?'

George shrugged. 'I reckoned whoever was writing these letters was chancing his arm. I expect he, or she, sent one to everyone.'

'Would it surprise you to learn that Timothy Grant had three such slips in the left pocket of his jeans, together with a letter addressed to Sergeant Skipwith here?'

'I'd love to know what it said!'

Dyle almost smiled. 'Or that we found a heap of chopped-up newspapers in Mr Grant's suitcase, under his bed.'

George shook his head. 'I'm very sorry to hear that. But no, it doesn't altogether surprise me. Tim had had a very disappointing career, which had left him quite embittered. He was certainly on my list of suspects, in so far as I gave the matter any thought at all.'

'He was here under an assumed name?'

'Yes. I have explained that twice already.'

Dyle made a note. 'We do need to get these details straight. When did you discover Miss Morny was your sister?'

'I've told you. During rehearsals.'

'You were sleeping with her at the time?'

'Yes.'

'And you've told us that you have slept with her once since.'

'I'm trying to be honest with you.'

'Believe me, we do appreciate it.'

'We certainly do.' Skipwith was comfortably aware that they already had enough on tape for a conviction for incest. And that would only be the start.

'When did Mr Grant find out?'

'Find out?'

'That you were committing incest.'

'I don't think he ever did.'

Skipwith snorted. 'That's what he saw, wasn't it?'

'Not here,' said George. 'There was nothing to see here.'

There was a tap at the door, and one of the constables put an anxious face round, beckoning to Dyle.

'I'll leave you with these two colleagues,' said Dyle, and slipped outside. If Skipwith would have preferred to be à deux, he couldn't show it in front of the constable. All three of them stayed silent until the Chief Inspector returned.

'When we started,' he said to George, 'I advised you of your rights, including the right to have a solicitor present. It seems that Colonel Bolitho has his own solicitor here, Mr Roger Bullivant, who is outside, and who is retained to act on your behalf. If you would like to confer with him, I can switch this tape off and suspend the interview.'

George shook his head. 'What I've told you was in the interests of trying to help you. I've no wish to get more people involved in all this. I'm innocent. I don't need a lawyer.'

Dyle smiled. 'As you wish. Tell me what your theory of these three deaths is. After all,' he added sardonically, 'no one's been closer to them than you have.'

George acknowledged the thrust with a slight grin. 'I think you've got a homicidal lunatic loose.'

'Any candidates?'

George's eyes strayed momentarily to Skipwith, who

was grinding his teeth beside the bookcase. 'What would be the pattern? Obsessive? Violent? Of limited intelligence? Very hard to find someone like that round here!' He smiled guilelessly at the infuriated Sergeant.

'Do you know?' said Dyle reflectively. 'I've decided I'm going to let you go. Everything you say makes sense to me. But I shouldn't like you to stray from the grounds for the time being. Is that agreed?'

'Of course!' George's principal emotion was surprise, though it was closely allied with relief.

'You *know* we'd get a conviction,' said Skipwith furiously after George had left. 'With incest on top of everything else, the jury'd be bound to find against him.'

'Maybe we would,' said Dyle thoughtfully. 'And maybe we still will. He's certainly on very dodgy ground. But we're not here just to get convictions. We want to find the right culprit, don't we?'

Skipwith didn't reply.

Chapter Twenty-Four

As soon as George had left the Library, he made his way quietly upstairs and locked himself in his bedroom. But within five minutes, he heard tapping on the door and opened it to admit Rose.

'I'm so relieved!' she said, hugging him.

'That they've released me?'

'That too,' she said, ingenuously. He shot her a quick, anxious glance. 'Now we've got to solve this case for them, and soon. Otherwise they'll have you back again.'

'Why do you say that?'

'Mr Bullivant says there's enough evidence for there to be a real risk of your getting convicted. They've let you go because the Chief Inspector doesn't think you did it.'

'His helpmate would like to nail me for something!'

'That's why we've got to act fast. I've sent Mr Bullivant to London to get a firm I know about to investigate everything about Mr Hammerson. That's the murder that matters.'

'How do you mean?' He was puzzled by her sudden forcefulness.

'Why would anyone murder Mrs Tregeare? She hadn't any money. She wasn't in anyone's way.'

'You mean?'

'She knew something. She'd seen something. She

probably didn't even know what it was. My bet is she saw someone doing something apparently innocuous. But that someone, the murderer, knew that if Mrs Tregeare ever mentioned what she'd seen, others would put two and two together.'

'I see.' He was fascinated. 'And Tim?'

'Who?'

'Tino, then.'

'Shall I tell you my theory?'

He laughed. 'I don't know how I'd stop you!'

'I think he wrote the anonymous letters.'

George stared. 'You're right,' he said. 'But do you mean you've had one too?'

'Hasn't everyone?'

'I don't know,' he replied. 'Nobody's talked about it.'

'Well, they wouldn't, would they? Not if they're remotely on target.'

'What did yours say?' She blushed and shook her head. 'Come on!'

She took a piece of paper out of the pocket of her jeans. It read:

Don't kid yourself he loves you. He
just wants your money and an easy poke.

He stared at it. 'Tasteful.'

'Quite.' She didn't dare say more.

'Well, you're quite right that Tim wrote these. They found all the bits and pieces in his room.'

'What did yours say?' She kept her eyes on his, watching his expression.

'Mine?' He laughed. 'Mine said, "I saw you".'

'I *knew* it!' she cried triumphantly. 'It had to be something like that.'

'I don't get it.'

'But it's obvious. Where there was something horrid

to say, he said it. Where there was nothing, he fell back on the old faithful: "I saw you." Doesn't say what he saw. Everyone's got something to hide. It could have been us kissing, or anything.'

'So?'

'So! To the murderer, such a message would spell potential disaster.'

'You mean . . .' George was digesting this slowly, 'if the murderer had received a similar message, he'd have panicked.'

'Yes! And if he'd sussed out Tino, there's your motive. Or rather she.'

'She?'

'I think so.' She sounded very smug.

'Why she?'

'Because only a woman could have got Tino's clothes off. He wasn't gay, was he?'

George shook his head. 'You're going too fast. He wasn't anything, that I ever saw. He might have gone for sex with either. That sort do, in my experience.'

'What a strange world you live in,' she said, gazing at him. 'You seem to accept it all quite calmly.'

George smiled. 'I suppose I've got used to it. I have to say it wasn't all that different in the wine trade.'

'You were in the wine trade?'

'Rose,' he said, taking her hands. 'Let's stick to catching the murderer first. Then I'll tell you about the wine trade.'

She nodded her agreement. 'So, if I'm right about Tino, and I'm sure I am, why murder Hammerson?'

'Why not murder him is a far more testing question.'

'Maybe so,' she said repressively. 'But—'

'Money,' he said quickly. 'Blackmail. Self-defence.'

'Self-defence with a six-foot broadsword?'

'Perhaps Hammerson had the sword?'

'Nonsense. Who benefited from his death?'

He grimaced. 'Isabelle. Mrs Hammerson. That's about it.'

She nodded. 'That's certainly how it seems.'

'I know it wasn't Isabelle.'

'Family solidarity?' She was smiling.

'Well, I don't believe it was Mrs Hammerson either.'

'Why not?'

'Instinct.'

'And who does your musician's instinct tell you did do it?'

'Winston.'

'The black baritone?'

'That's him.'

'Colour prejudice?'

'Certainly not. But a man who lets me rehearse him as Leporello when he hasn't got a work permit is capable of absolutely anything.'

'What we need to do,' she said, still fizzing with energy, 'is to try to identify anything unique or unusual that happened or that people said.'

'Or did?'

She looked hard at him. 'Have you something in mind?'

'Well.' He shuffled his feet. 'In the interval, when I went to the Gents, it had odd things in it. Violet tissues, a box of sanitary towels. That struck me as odd.'

'Very odd,' she agreed.

'And that old crazy woman . . .'

'Poppie Pencarrow?'

'I think so. She tried to come into the Gents twice, even though there was a huge sign.'

'She's as blind as a bat.'

He pursed his lips. 'But I saw Isabelle coming out of the Ladies . . .'

'Where Hammerson was found, by you.'

'Quite, but she said it was the Gents.'

'So why was she in there – or shouldn't I ask?'

'She said there was a fat drunk woman hogging the Ladies, who winked at her.'

Rose giggled. 'Agatha Orchard! Must have been. She's always winking at people. Dad says it used to get her into all sorts of trouble. Before she got fat.'

'Does she drink?'

'Like a fish.'

'There you are then.'

She grabbed his hands. 'Don't you see what this means?'

'Means?'

'Yes! *Think!* Someone must have swapped the signs.'

'As a joke?'

'No, for a good reason. For the murder.'

'But why?'

'I don't know,' she said, suddenly dispirited. 'Let's go and look.'

'The room was sealed.'

'Not any more. They took away a lot of that stripy tape this afternoon.'

Together they hurried along the corridor and down the stairs. There was loud chatter from the kitchen, and the hum of computers from the Dining Room. Creeping between the two, they reached the two lavatories, both with identical panelled wooden doors, the first where the body had been found, and the second which George had used as the Gents.

'Next door to each other,' said Rose. 'No reason to choose one rather than the other.'

'Suppose you're right,' said George. 'This first door must originally have been the Gents. And the second was the Ladies.'

'With violet tissues and STs.' She smiled.

'Exactly. But the murderer ...'

'Or murderess ...'

184

'If you must,' he conceded. 'Whoever. They wanted to lure Hammerson to his death. Surely he'd have been more likely to go into the Gents?'

'Not if he was meeting a woman,' pointed out Rose triumphantly. 'And expecting something rather nice when he did meet her. She'd say, "Come into the Ladies loo with me, darling, and I'll make you the luckiest man on earth." '

'With a six-foot sword?'

'That,' she explained patiently, 'was already in place. When was it last used?'

'In the very first scene.'

'And then put where?'

'God! I've explained all this to Laurel and Hardy in there about a hundred times.'

'So now explain it to me.'

'It got propped up in the Flower Room after they'd dragged the "body" out.'

'So anyone could have snatched it, run round the outside of the house, and popped it behind the door?'

He paused to consider. 'It'd be an awful risk. But it *could* be done.'

'It was!' she said with great confidence.

He opened the second door. 'They're identical, aren't they? I don't see the point.'

'George! Come back here!' She was shouting with excitement from next door. '*Look!* Do you see?'

'I do see.' There was a rather obvious difference. For this room had a window, high up, but quite large enough to use as an exit.

Chapter Twenty-Five

'There you are!' Jane looked delighted to see them together. 'We're all agreed on the school performance. Mrs Hammerson will give everyone fifty pounds cash as a present, and Alison is going to cook something sumptuous for us before the rehearsal.'

'That sounds nice,' said George, impatient at being interrupted at such a point.

'We want you to reconnoitre. There's a small stage, apparently. Alison will take you over now.'

'Fine.' He glanced at Rose.

'I'm going to speak to Mr Dyle,' she said, and hurried away down the corridor.

'Lovely girl,' said Jane. 'Just right for you.'

'Piss off!' He went to join Hammerson's secretary who was waiting by her car in the front courtyard.

It took three minutes to reach Tredinnick Primary School by Porsche.

'Do you always drive like that?'

Alison laughed. 'Only when I know there's no one coming the other way!'

'Lead on.'

The school was a low brick building with two arched doorways, one marked 'Boys' and the other 'Girls', and the date 1903 was incised between the two. There was also a metal plaque announcing that the building had been opened by The Lady Matilda Bolitho, Chairman of Governors.

'This is the assembly hall.'

It was nearly forty feet long, with a raised stage and faded green velvet curtains at one end, and a battery of tin food trolleys drawn up in ranks at the other. It smelt the same as the Taunton establishment.

'Any changing rooms?'

'Only one of the classrooms.'

'That'll do. These doors are rather low.' He'd nearly hit his head on one.

'Try stooping.' There was something very attractive about her personality. It was so open, and without side. Nor was he entirely indifferent to her trim figure.

'Do you always come down for weekends?'

She grinned. 'It *was* part of my job. I'll be reassigned now. With any luck, I'll get a boss who lives a bit nearer London!'

'Ow!' He did hit his head this time. 'They must have small teachers in Cornwall. Though I must warn the others. I don't want any wigs coming unstuck.'

'Like Maria's, you mean?'

'Yes, indeed!' George laughed. 'That was really funny, wasn't it?'

'She didn't look as though she thought so,' said Alison judiciously.

'Perhaps not, but that's the risk in live entertainment. Where are the loos?'

'Over here.' She really knew her way around. It was a relief to him, used to working with singers who, on tour, seemed to develop the corporate helplessness of newborn babies, to find himself working alongside a fellow professional.

*

As soon as they got back to Bolitho, Rose rushed out to grab him. 'Quick!' she said, and led him away to the Tapestry Room.

'What?'

'I've been thinking about that window.'

'In the lavatory?'

'Yes!'

'What about it?'

'You found the body, didn't you?'

'Yes.'

'Is it true he was sitting on the lavatory seat?'

'More or less.'

'Come with me.' She dragged him back past the stairs and down the corridor to the room where Hammerson had died. 'If the body's on the loo, how would you get out of that window?'

'I'd . . .' He stared. 'I see,' he said. 'Not easy.'

'What is?' enquired Dyle, who had emerged from the second lavatory.

'We think,' said Rose impulsively, 'that the murderer lured Hammerson in here and then escaped through that window.'

Dyle smiled down at her. 'Good,' he said. 'Because that's what I think too.'

'But in that case . . .' George was struggling with his thoughts. 'They must have had to step up on Hammerson, on his *head*.'

'So what we want to know, Chief Inspector,' persisted Rose, 'is, was there any sign of bruising or tearing on his face or head?'

'There was,' he said gravely, and with a certain respect.

'Pronounced or light?'

He grinned. 'Light,' he said. 'Now I suggest you leave the police work to us.'

'Do you have a suspect?' she demanded. 'Other than poor Mr Sinclair here?'

Dyle preserved a face of intractable blandness. 'I just pursue facts, miss,' he said. 'Like the fact that someone paid four thousand pounds into poor Mr Sinclair here's bank account this morning.'

George stared at him. 'Four thousand pounds! Into my account?'

The tall policeman nodded. 'Perhaps Miss Bolitho can explain,' he said helpfully, and left a very embarrassed Rose to admit to trying to help him in the most practical way she knew.

Chapter Twenty-Six

It was at the lunch, cooked by Alison, *filet de boeuf en croûte* with many trimmings, before the rehearsal next day, that Isabelle dropped her bombshell. George had just, without looking at her, spooned some more roast potatoes on to her plate when she said: 'It's exciting, isn't it?'

'What is, dear?' Mrs Bolitho had taken a rather unexpected fancy to Isabelle, who had taught her the names of some obscure Bourbon roses in the cutting border.

'Wondering if they'll find out.'

'Find out what?' asked Bruno with his mouth full. It was remarkable how his fads faded away in the face of the smell of good cooking.

'Who did it, of course.'

'The murders?'

'Well,' she crunched happily on a crispy piece of potato, '*the* murder. The only successful one, I mean. The others were failures, weren't they?'

'I don't know,' said Ed impatiently, being at the wrong end of the table for what was left of the horse-radish. 'You tell us.'

'Wouldn't that be rather dangerous?' she enquired with mock naïveté.

'Only if you know who did it.' The other conversations were dying away.

'*Of course* I know who did it!' she said. 'I thought everyone did.'

'If that's a joke,' said Mrs Hammerson, who was sitting between the Colonel and Rose further down the table, 'I consider it in the worst possible taste.' She stood up, flung down her napkin and walked out, white-faced.

'I must say . . .' The Colonel was, frankly, out of his depth.

'She's only joking,' said George furiously, 'to see your faces.'

'And what did you see in our faces?' enquired Jane, interested.

'What I expected,' was the gnomic reply. 'Georges,' Isabelle, well satisfied to hold the undivided attention of the whole room, held out a long white hand to him, 'will you come and run through "Batti, batti" with me before we go to the school. Thank you for a wonderful lunch,' she said to Alison, who had lived up to her promise. '*Au revoir, mes enfants!*' She all but danced out of the room, followed by a sheepish George.

As soon as they were in the Saloon, he grabbed her by the wrists and swung her round.

'You idiot!'

She flapped her eyes at him. 'Oh, *chéri*! Is this to be rape?' She pushed herself against him. 'I hope so. I miss your body.'

'No, you don't!' he snapped. 'I heard you the night of the storm. *Éventrez-moi!*' Yet still he held her close to him, breathing in her scent as if with his last gasp.

'And you?' She smiled up at him, wriggling her hips. 'Have you not been consoling yourself with that Cornish pygmy? The one who gives you money.'

'*Isabelle!*'

Her eyes flashed. 'I knew it! What hypocrites men are. For you it is an innocent pastime, but with us it is betrayal.'

'Anyway,' he thrust her away, 'are you mad? What was that nonsense about the murders?'

'Practicalities, *mon ami*. If I am not to lose you for the next thirty years, I think I had better unmask the villain.'

'You mean you *don't* know who did it?'

She shrugged. 'Of course not. But maybe whoever did thinks I know. And if so . . .'

'He'll murder you. A *brilliant* move.'

'It is not easy to murder someone who expects it.'

He put his hands round her throat and squeezed, squeezed so tight that her face turned red and her legs, kicking out at first, began to flail feebly. 'You see?' he said when she had regained her breath. 'It could have been me.'

'Yes,' she gasped, still red in the face, and then drove her knee hard between his legs. 'See,' she lay down beside him, 'I share your English sense of humour, *con*.'

'Very funny.' The pain was excruciating.

'Now,' she pulled him to his feet, ' "Batti, batti". And then you will keep an eye on your Isabelle?'

'I will.' He limped to the piano, and she began to sing. Neither of them was aware of a third presence, a single eye, pressed to the slit where the door to the Tapestry Room remained ajar, coldly appraising the scene.

Chapter Twenty-Seven

The school rehearsal had been scheduled for four-thirty, to give the caretaker time to clear up after the seniors had left. But by the time everyone was assembled, having walked down from Bolitho, it was nearer six.

The audience consisted of the two Bolitho women (the Colonel having stayed behind, ostensibly to watch over the house though perhaps also to watch the boxing on television), Mrs Hammerson, Alison Cook, Dyle, Skipwith and, on his own at the back, ignoring the others' hostility, the shambling figure of Alan Waterhouse. The last two days had played havoc with his hygiene, and he did not appear to have shaved very thoroughly.

The piano was up on the narrow stage, and the troupe could only manage a part of Jane's staging with a four-foot abyss into the stalls where they would normally have been in mid-stride. Nevertheless the show sped along as usual. Maria forgot her part in the trio, Bruno coughed in his serenade and Jane cracked in 'Mi tradi'. In short, the Floria Tosca Grand Opera Company in full flow. Even the smoke machine managed a creditable fog of vapour, which gave George an anxious moment when he realized he couldn't see Isabelle in the wings. But through she came, having waited as usual for Ed to accomplish his quick change from Commendatore back to Masetto and the opera finished to some quite enthusiastic applause, especially from Chief Inspector Dyle.

'My congratulations!' He was beaming at Maria. 'A wonderful rendition.'

She beamed back. 'Thank you. Thank you.'

'No, I assure you. Quite wonderful.'

A policewoman had hurried in and now handed him a folded sheet of paper. He read it carefully, handed it to Skipwith without comment, and asked George when everyone would be returning to Bolitho Court.

'Now,' said George.

'Will you be driving?'

'No. We'll walk back.' It had taken them less than ten minutes by the coastal path.

'Then I'll walk with you.' His face held nothing beyond a polite desire to please.

It was already quite dark when they came down the steps of the school and crossed the tarmac playground. There was a small concrete path that led through some bushes and this then petered out into the gravelly footpath that skirted the cliffs. George had been walking for quite four minutes when he suddenly stopped to check on Isabelle. She was nowhere to be seen.

'Where's Isabelle?' he asked Ed, who was carrying a sack of costumes.

'She said she'd come with Rose.'

'Where's Rose?'

'I'm here!' She came up through the mist, smiling tenderly.

'Have you seen Isabelle?'

Her smile faded. 'Yes. I gave her the school key. She wanted to practise her aria again.'

'What?' He began to run, pounding back along the path, heedless of shouting behind.

The bushes loomed – he almost vaulted them but, tripping, banged his face painfully against the concrete.

Dimly he could hear her voice, the golden notes spilling over into the cadenza. He clambered back to his feet. Someone was close behind him. He pelted across the playground, and pulled open the swing door. Isabelle, her hands clenched, was facing him on the platform, having just completed the aria. And then, as George watched, a shadow slipped out from behind the green velvet curtain and towards Isabelle. Even in that dim light, he knew it was Alison. She was holding a long kitchen knife and, as he shouted, she raised it to plunge into Isabelle's unsuspecting back. There was a shattering explosion behind him, and to his horror, Alison's face seemed to dissolve, to blur, spattering the screaming Isabelle with blood as her assailant, lifeless, slid, so slowly, to the floor. Turning, his ears still ringing, he saw Rose just behind him, her pistol held firm and straight with both avenging hands. The thing he was always to remember afterwards was the overpowering stench of cordite.

Rose's father ran towards her, as George ran to Isabelle. 'What a shot!' cried the Colonel proudly. 'I couldn't have done better myself.'

'It's funny,' said Rose slowly, her face expressing anything but comedy, 'but I wish to God I'd missed.'

Chapter Twenty-Eight

'I still don't understand.' Colonel Bolitho was sitting in his wing-chair safely back beside the smouldering Library fire, staring at Rose and George, together on the sofa. Dyle and a decidedly disappointed Skipwith had left with their team. All trace that for nearly a week, Bolitho Court had been at the centre of a major police investigation, had finally and gratefully been expunged. 'You mean that Alison Cook killed them all?'

George nodded.

'But in God's name, why? Why kill poor Mrs Tregeare?'

'Mrs Tregeare was killed because she saw something. It all started at our first performance of *Don Giovanni*. We all knew Clay Hammerson was there, because we saw him in the front row, drooling over Isabelle. What we didn't know was that Alison was also there.'

'Because she was having an affair with him?'

'Exactly. That's what put me on to her.'

'When she laughed about Maria's accident?'

'Yes. There was no reason why she shouldn't have been at our first night, in Hammerson's party, as his secretary.'

'At Almondsbury?'

'Yes. Yet she was so insistent that she hadn't been there. And I had another reference. When Lord Harrogate said someone wanted to meet her, he said something to me about that being "brave". It didn't make any sense at the time. But, recently, thinking back on it, I realized it could mean the man's current squeeze was also around then. That's when I started thinking about her motive. As his current mistress, she would have made sure she'd been in his Will. As his secretary, she would have known how often he changed it. And when she saw Isabelle coming up in the fast lane—'

'She thought she'd better act even faster,' broke in Rose. 'Though in fact she was already too late.'

The Colonel chuckled. 'That man must have changed his Will once a month!'

'Money meant everything to her,' went on George, 'even though she was very well paid. So she changed the signs on the lavatories—'

'In order to be able to escape through the window if she got blood on her clothes,' put in Rose.

'And Mrs Tregeare must have seen something . . .'

'I'm very much afraid,' said Mary Bolitho, who had entered the room silently, and had been listening in the doorway, 'that that may have been my fault. I'd been looking for the screwdriver, you know, dear, the only one that's strong enough to shift the screws on the old cabinet. It wasn't in its normal place. That dreadful woman was there when I asked poor Mrs Tregeare about it and I thought at the time that there was something odd between them. Of course I never gave it another thought, but now I think back, I believe she did mutter something and then she shut up. What induced her to say nothing I can't imagine.'

'Servants' solidarity, knowing Mrs Tregeare,' said Rose sadly. 'She would have accepted Alison as a servant, because that's how the Hammersons treated her. She was such a *militant*, wasn't she, Dad? She'd never have told anything against another member of staff, not ever. And it killed her.'

The Colonel was filling his pipe, and nodded ruefully. 'She had very strong views,' he said. 'A fine Celt, in every way.' Now that she was dead, it seemed to him wrong to recall her extraordinary mania for spoiling perfectly good bacon.

'The one thing I still don't understand,' said George, 'is that dreadful sound in the Saloon ceiling. Rose said there's some family tradition of the house mourning the approaching death of a Bolitho.' He felt absurd even mentioning such an idea. 'Nothing happened, but the noise was real enough. I do think you should get a joiner to have a look.'

The Colonel sucked at his pipe. 'Deirdre Tregeare,' he said quietly, 'was a Bolitho too. I always knew that. She was my grandfather's girl. He had a bit of a fling with one of the housemaids. I don't know if she ever knew. She was brought up in the village, of course, but I used to wonder if that's why she took such a pride in the old place.'

'You never told me that!' said Mary Bolitho, intrigued.

'No.' The Colonel showed no inclination to add to what he had already said. They sat in silence for a minute or so.

At last Mary Bolitho said, 'And Tim, or Tino, or whatever name he went by?'

'He had no one to blame but himself,' said George. 'I expect he just sent one too many poison-pen letters. Most people threw them away, as I did. But he frightened Alison enough for her to kill him.'

'I even had one myself,' said the Colonel, colouring slightly.

'*Billy!* You never said.'

'Certainly not!' He coughed, embarrassed. 'Filthy muck.'

'What did it say?' Mary Bolitho certainly wasn't going to let the matter rest there.

198

'A lot of nonsense.' He had turned a quite alarming colour.

'I know!' cried Rose triumphantly. 'It was about Maria, wasn't it?' Her father's nose was almost indigo with embarrassment.

'*Billy!* You weren't flirting with her?'

'Certainly not!' said the old soldier robustly. 'Fine-looking woman, but not my type.'

'I should hope not,' said his comparatively minuscule wife. 'That great tub of lard . . .'

The Colonel opened his mouth, caught his daughter's eye, and closed it again.

'It only needed Isabelle's idiotic little trap, and there we were,' put in George tactfully.

'Well, I think it was very plucky of that blonde girl . . . er . . . Isabelle,' said Mrs Bolitho. 'She might have been killed.' A silence fell in the room.

'But she wasn't,' said Rose, and the second silence lasted even longer.

After a bit, Mrs Bolitho caught her husband's eye. 'Time for us to be sorting out your papers.'

'My papers? What papers?' She gave him a truly ferocious look. 'Eh? Oh! *Those* papers!' He'd never been good at codes, even coming last in his section at the staff college in Quetta. Cramming his pipe into his pocket, he rose awkwardly and stumbled out in pursuit of his wife.

'I don't think my father would have been a success on the stage,' said Rose softly, after the door had closed.

George grunted. He had a lump in his throat which was making speech difficult.

'You're going, aren't you? No! Don't answer.' She got up and went round to stand behind him, her hands on his shoulders, so that he shouldn't see her tears. 'I know you love her. I *do* understand.' He was shaking his head, and raised one hand to hold on to her. 'My father was afraid you wanted my money. And you know you can have it, willingly.' He shook his head even more violently. 'It means nothing to me, without you.'

'I...' It was no good. Tears were streaming down his face. He couldn't say a word.

'Hush.' She bent down and, very tenderly, kissed the top of his head. 'I'll always love you.'

'Please,' he said painfully. 'Don't...'

'Yes,' she said. 'And I'll be here, if you need me. I know you can't stay. Life on the road is a powerful rival, too powerful for me. No!' She checked him again, as he tried to turn round, to face her. 'I'm going upstairs now. I want this to be our goodbye.' And she ran out of the door, slamming it behind her.

For a long, long time, he sat there, staring at the spitting logs. Then he heard the sound of tyres on the gravel, and Isabelle's voice in the hall, calling him.